THE FLOWER KING

LESLEY HOWARTH

WALKER BOOKS
AND SUBSIDIARIES
LONDON · BOSTON · SYDNEY

First published 1993 by Walker Books Ltd
87 Vauxhall Walk, London SE11 5HJ

This edition published 2000

2 4 6 8 10 9 7 5 3 1

This book has been typeset in Sabon.

Printed in Great Britain by
Cox & Wyman Ltd, Reading, Berkshire

British Library Cataloguing in Publication Data
A catalogue record for this book is
available from the British Library.

The characters in this book are entirely fictitious and
bear no relation to any person alive or dead.

ISBN 0-7445-7719-5

For
Kay and Don

CHAPTER ONE

Take it from me, red's trouble. Any kind of red. The colours to watch out for are: red, orange, purple, brown and black. Red's a panic button, black's a cruising shark. Orange, purple and brown are all mixtures, and bound to be tricky.

Orange isn't good or bad, but it's never what it seems. Never trust anyone giving you orange. As far as yellow goes – and clear, bright yellow's pretty unusual – as far as yellow goes, it hopes for the best. Green's a feelgood colour, the best of all; if someone sends me green I just stand there and soak it up.

Light blue is refuge from the storm – sort of calm and neutral; too much, and it makes me sad inside, the kind of sadness you get when you think too much about the past. Dark blue's best avoided. You can get hitched up in indigo. Dark blue feels sorry for itself, and it's far too close to purple for comfort.

Purple's the person at a party who won't join in, because purple thinks it's special. Bit cruel, too. Watch out for it. Brown's a mixture of everything else, and it can mean almost anything. Where it's friendly-dog brown it'll never let you down – and where it isn't, it muddies everything up and gets in the way. Like grey. Grey's just a nuisance.

And white? No one ever yet sent me white light. If they ever did, I'm sure I would remember.

I always *could* feel colours. Or colour feelings, whichever way you want to look at it. One day when I was four, M told me the family dog had been taken off to live on a farm (where he would be much happier), when, in fact, he'd been splatted on the filling station forecourt by an incoming delivery lorry. Her face as she told the tale gave me tricky orange through anxious red; and orange, as I said before, is *not* a colour to be trusted.

Every month there were delivery lorries. But there were no more family dogs after Stud, even though D said the garage and stores needed security. Instead, D – that's my dad – installed video cameras on the forecourt. He put two in the shop as well, as the business grew. Dawe's Filling Station, some said, had grown like a blister. Not everyone likes D. Even I don't like him sometimes.

We open seven to nine every day of the year except Christmas Day, and almost everyone in the village uses the pumps, and almost everyone who uses the pumps uses the stores. Once Rene left, a lot more people came in. Rene never smiled. She served customers like something had just died under her nose. No one was sorry when she took her hatchet face off out of it at last, and ruined someone else's day. After Rene there was Nikki and Carol, and after them Shirley and a woman with bad teeth called Net. Then it was Jean – I was sorry when she left – and Sue. At the moment it's Gwen and Lorraine, on a four-day rota. Saturdays, I help on the video hire. Or I go up Needham's with M to see Pinny and Uncle Champion.

Uncle Champion's been three years at Needham's Green Residential Home, out to Redmoor. He's my great-uncle – M's father's brother. Been in dry stone walling most of his life. Most of the walls – or 'edges – around the village owe something to Jack Champion. Several chapels, as well. Now he's hedged in himself at Needham's Green, in his woofy chair by the alcove. We go and see him most Saturdays, I don't know why, since Uncle Champion gives off tides of purple-brown, which is "bog off and leave me be" plain as speaking. But Saturdays at Needham's was how I came to know Pinny. She's just an old lady I talk to when we visit Uncle Jack – sits left of the telly by the dividing doors usually, so's you have to walk round her all the time; but it's Pinny makes Saturdays what they are.

I knew yellow was important when I was telling Pinny about Rumbold's Funpark last Saturday, so I knew daffs would hit the spot. I decided then and there I'd get her a faceful of yellow to dip her old beak in and come up silly with pollen. Then we'd have yellow between us, as well as everything else.

Usually her nose is purple, not yellow. Mrs Pinder – I call her Pinny – has bad circulation. The day lounge at Needham's is always hot as a bakehouse – the whole place is – but still her legs are plum-skin purple. Sometimes I think they keep it hot to irritate them, though most of 'em are pretty irritable anyway.

Last Saturday, in the day lounge, I said, "Why's it always so hot in here?"

"Tin't hot," said Pinny. "I'm cold."

"You're always cold," I said, because she is. Then I went on with Rumbold's Funpark. "After, we went on the Snake. Looks rubbish but it's dynamite on the bends. I thought it'd be naff but Jamie Tree said it goes a bit –"

Pinny fidgeted her hands on her day blanket. Mrs Dingle's day blanket, it was. Probably why she looked so jumpy. There'd be hell up if dizzy Dingle caught her with the blue blanket.

"Get on," said Pinny, and I knew what she wanted. She wanted me to be eyes again; so I had to stop and think a moment exactly what the Snake Ride at Rumbold's was like so's I could tell it the way she liked me to, as if she'd been there herself. That was being eyes. Pinny's were good for filching blankets but not much else, being as they never went anywhere or saw anything. I had to be eyes and legs for Pinny, because she didn't get out much, hardly at all. The hairdresser came Wednesdays and the chiropodist once a month to pare her horny old feet – but the rest of the time nothing much happened to tell of, and Pinny stopped where she was in Needham's Green and didn't miss much at all except freedom and chip shop chips, which I bring her sometimes on the sly. Now and again I bring her a bit of second-hand freedom as well. That's being eyes, but it has to be good. No messing, with Pinny.

"The Snake Ride's about three or four loops—"

"Tell it three, then? Or four?"

"Four. You're in this train an' the front bit's got up like a snake's head. The ride's flat to start, then round and up slowly, then *really* fast round and down so it almost tears your head off. Then round fast again so you think you're flyin' off the rails, and through to the start again. And you get – four times round each go. Then there's the log flume. And the drop slide. Which d'you want?"

Pinny screwed up her eyes. It gave me a chance to check the damage. Bit more hair gone on the left-hand side of her head, where the bump was. And some nasty carpet burn.

M said Mrs Screech said she was a menace with that walking frame, Mrs Pinder. Top landing, she fell from. Mrs Screech said that that was an end of it, and Pinny's walking frame was shut away for good now. She'd only tried to get up top landing on her own, no one knew why. Probably it was because of Miss Cuthburt.

Pinny had had it in for Miss Cuthburt a long time over the talc. I *told* her I wasn't turning Miss Cuthburt's room over for her lily of the valley talc because she'd probably just lost it somewhere. I told her Miss Cuthburt didn't *have* her dozy talc, but she wouldn't have it. I can just see her now, going up one stair at a time like grim death to turn out Cath-Cuth's drawers. Catherine Cuthburt, who held herself so tight and trim she stuck like a splinter in Pinny's eye, with her cardigan done up close, every button, under her waste-not-want-not chin.

"Drop slide," said Pinny, popping open again.

When I started to tell it, it was then I got the yellow. Yellow light around the day room, yellow off the naff rug by the storage heater, off the curtains, the mirror, the magazine rack, yellow off the back of Uncle Champion's stinky chair, off the oranges in the bowl on the telly and the ends of old Christmas streamers, flopping in the draught from the dining room door. Yellow all around – and while I was telling the drop slide, yellow in Pinny's head, I could feel it, while her purple paws jumped on dizzy Dingle's blanket and she fell twenty foot with me down the drop slide at Rumbold's Funpark and fetched up spinning in the scoop, with her stomach left behind up top with mine.

And everything that *was* yellow in that room jumped out at me like a signal. I could tell you everything yellow in that room now, from the pattern in the carpet to the end of Mrs Rhapson's crochet hook in the wool beside her yellow laxative bullets. It sharpened me up, that yellow, and I knew then it was a thread of something clear and bright in Pinny's story. It was then I remembered the flower field. Daffs, I thought. Daffs for Pinny, that's what.

There they were. You can't miss 'em, coming down the dip in the lane – a blazing field of yellow, as though someone came in the night and laid a carpet on the hill for a laugh. I lost them again coming up Jago's Cross, then round on the village road. But when I got in the gate I made a picture in my head for Pinny, the field was so brave and bright with a thousand thousand yellow flowers. It was brilliant, that daffodil field – brilliant like a big ship or anything else big that fills you up. I felt like clapping. Instead I slicked up between the rows and made a start.

"Mee–oo," called the buzzard hawks, "Mee–oo." They've got a nest in the oak on the far hedge. I never go by the flower field without checking the sky for a wheeling boomerang shape over the Valley, but I'd never yet had a good look. The shapes were always razor-thin, kite-high.

The daffodil rows ran away down over the hill like streamers. In the middle of the field stood an easel and someone in a big hat, painting. I worked my way over slowly, picking as I went. The sappy daffodil stalks bled gunk all over me, more than you'd ever think, so I was wishing for a carrier bag or anything to put them in by the time I reached the picture.

The picture was brave as the field; lardy blobs of yellow with purple hills and mine-stacks up behind, all worked on what looked like a bit of old hardboard.

The hat turned. Straight away, I felt guilty. But "Hello there," she said, squinting over her hardboard. She sighed and shook her head. "I can't get 'em. They're too hard."

Her face was keen and brown. Her floppy hat and her fuzzy hair and her long clothes were brown, too; but her thumb was green – green to the knuckle where she held her board for mixing on – her palette. It was messed all over with shiny wormcasts of orange-red and sticky blue and spoilt yellow.

The daffodils rippled like wheat as the wind ran over the hill. I could see the problem. She might as well've drenched her picture-board in yellow to start, as pick and pad it yellow by degrees. But it was a great idea. Standing painting in the middle of a sea of daffodils, it was a great idea. I was glad someone else felt the same way I did about the field. What did it matter how many score bunches were bundled – or not – for market? The glory was, the field itself. I felt like rolling in all that yellow. I might've, if she hadn't been there, dibbing and dabbing. But she was.

"They're gone, these," I said guiltily. "Just as well pick 'em, Roland said. Roland said, only buds for market."

"Roland?"

"Roland Boyton. Rents the field. *Did* rent it, anyway."

"Yes," she nodded, brown and friendly. "Just as well pick 'em." Friendly brown – that was what she was sending. No yellow behind *her* eyes. Plenty in front, but none behind.

15

Only friendly brown, fogging her face a moment.

"They'd have cleared these by now years ago," she said.

"Bottom's gone out of the market. Roland said he could've sold as many as he could've got picked a fortnight ago. But now everyone got their stuff to market, the bottom's gone. Take a carful if you want, Roland said."

She took up green; dabbed and looked, looked and dabbed. A green trickle zigzagged down her thumb and plopped in her workbox, jammed tight with rags and brushes and gummy tubes of colour.

"All the fields around were under flowers years ago. Flowers, far as you can see," she said. "Hard to believe now, isn't it?"

I scanned around. The bland green barley fields looked back. "I guess," I nodded. "I never really thought."

"Narcissus, daffs of every kind, gentians, anemones ... strawberries too, of course. Scores of pickers at the height of the season, loading carts for the quay. Off they'd go, the flower barges, down the river to Tarmouth Market on the morning tide..." Her voice trailed away. She took up magenta. "A way of life. All gone."

"Yeh," I said. "These is all for the chop. Roland says, tin't worth his while renting the ground for planting. Father-in-law sold off the

16

field now, anyhow."

"Shame, too." She cocked her head. "*The Last Field* or *Golden Requiem*. Which d'you think?"

"Which what?"

"For a title. For the picture. *The Last Field* or—"

"Yes," I said quickly. "That's what it is, isn't it?"

I moved up close to the easel. She'd made the best of it she could. Only a madman would've tried to paint each flower. Instead, she'd caught the whole in a mash of cross-strokes. I narrowed my eyes over the field beyond. She had it, all right. It was very—

A shadow fell on the picture and I looked up.

They were trading places on the wind, one under another. Not one, but *both* buzzard hawks – not more than twenty feet over our heads. I held my breath.

Lower they dropped – and lower, and *never* had I seen them so close, and their wings were wider than I ever dreamed and flashed along with lightest beige, and their lion eyes scanned us both beneath and didn't care for anything but themselves. And they were *so* big. So much bigger than I'd thought, they seemed to shade the light away, so royal they took my breath away with it. Lower, I dared them – lower. Lower, lower – to me!

Suddenly they took the wind under their

wings. It snatched them away like leaves. We watched them ride the updraught over the hill, making height in easy circles. "Mee–oo," they called. "Mee–oo." At last they were thin as an eyelash, both – and then they were gone.

"*Wow!*" I said. "Why did they *do* that? Why did they come right *down* like that?"

But she was busy with a thin brush slicked in brown. Making a couple or two quick strokes like a Chinese signwriter, she stood away. There were the buzzard hawks, high in her cornflower blue sky, under the top right-hand corner of the painting.

"Yes," she said. "It'll do."

It would, too. It was the finishing touch. Or so I thought. She dibbled her brush in a pot on her easel and cuffed it clean with a rag.

"'I wandered lonely as a cloud'." She looked up wickedly under her hat. "'That floats on high o'er vales and hills…'"

I grinned. Someone had to say it. "'When all at once I saw a crowd, A host, of golden daffodils.'" It was one of Uncle Champion's favourite poems.

She grinned back. "Want a bag for your daffs?"

"Please. If you got one. They're for a friend," I added.

She gave me a carrier bag which smelt of turps. I stuffed in the daffs. "It's good," I said, "you paintin'. It's good you're painting 'em before they get the chop."

"I'm not done yet. Got to put in the last flower picker, yet. The very last."

I nodded. "G'bye," I called, when I was a little way away.

"Bye, now." She took up a wedge-shaped brush and turned away, flicking her hair on her shoulder.

All the way back I kept flashing on the moment the buzzard hawks had come howling down on our heads. The daffodils glowed yellow in the top of the bag as I bumped them along home. It was Pinny Pinder had thrown out all this yellow. There was something – something to do with Pinny. The buzzard hawks knew. Of course, it might've been a mouse or a shrew along the rows that had drawn them down to see. But all the same, I didn't think it was. For some reason, I thought it was me.

CHAPTER
TWO

I drowned Pinny's daffs in a bucket by the back door and wandered over the stores to find M. That's Mum, in case you're wondering. Lorraine was on the till. Lorraine could do at least three things at once. When she punched petrol on the till, called up the video hire records on the computer and weighed a bag of apples all at the same time, I wondered at the way she had of making things work for her. Lorraine was M's current linchpin. She knew where everything was, from batteries to Bisto.

"Where's Mum?" I asked.

"In back," said Lorraine smoothly, handing out change and shifting the video returns with her foot.

She wasn't, at all. She was gassing with Gwen over the end freezer. Or rather, humming:

"Dum-dum *dum* dum *dum* dum diddle-um—"

"No," said Gwen breathlessly, "*Der* duh-duh *der* duh-duh *der* der *der*—"

How did I guess? *The Defenders* theme *again*. *The Defenders* was a lame old Sixties show I'd been hearing about so much lately I could almost remember it myself.

"Then – " said Gwen, she was almost shouting – "then it's the sword on the black and white table, then—"

"Then John Gently throws down his glove," cut in M, "and Rhetta Zest—"

"In her catsuit—"

"In her catsuit, whips this shield off of the wall with – what was it, on the shield?"

"You know, 'The Defenders', the thing like a castle with 'The Defenders' over the top, and it goes: starring Howard Powell as John Gently and Camilla ... Camilla what's-her-face as Rhetta Zest. Then they cross swords and it goes to—"

"It goes to where they're on like the top of castle and she's got a big—"

"Eagle or something."

"A big eagle sat on her arm, and as it flies off, the rest of the names go up."

"When are we going up Needham's?" I asked quickly, before they could start again.

"What?" M wiped her eyes with a tissue. "Where've you been?"

"Down the daffodil field. There was a woman there. Painting."

M snorted. "That'd be Margaret Bath."

"What about Needham's?"

"What about it?" asked M shortly. "Howard Powell's opening Cletchley Fete this afternoon."

I knew then Pinny wouldn't get her daffs. They were all mad on Howard Powell since he'd moved in down the road. Supposedly he'd been a big noise in television back in the Sixties. The only thing I'd ever seen him in was a naff American cop show called *King's Bluff*. He filled up the whole screen. M said he'd been a lot thinner when he was John Gently in *The Defenders*. He didn't look as if he could defend a glass of milk, he just looked big and old.

Ever since the article in the local paper headed: "Defender Chooses Cletchley", M had left off wearing her nylon overall in the shop, just in case he popped in for a bottle of plonk. The picture in the paper had Howard Powell in front of Stopeley House. Stopeley House was a big old place overlooking the river between our village and Cletchley. Big noise Howard Powell had moved in a couple of months back, and had kept a low profile ever since. But no one in either village who could remember *The Defenders* had got over it yet. Howard Powell – *the* Howard Powell – up on Stopeley Rise. But then, you had to be at least forty to remember *The Defenders*.

"Well *I'm* going to Needham's," I said firmly. "I picked a load of daffodils for Pin—Mrs Pinder, and I'm going up there with them."

"I want you up the fete with me," said M, sending out warning stabs of purple-red the colour of dentist's mouthwash. "There's things I want carried."

Gwen moved off to the fruit and veg with her ears flapping. She lumped a few tired melons around.

"Uncle Champion won't like it," I grumbled. "We always go Saturdays. Flowers'll die by *next* Saturday."

"Uncle Champion can like it or lump it." M took up a price list and clapped her chest for a Biro. "Run up the till and get us a Biro. How many daffs you got?"

"Big bucketful."

"Split 'em up outside. Sixty pee for ten."

"But I got them for Pi—"

"And while you're up the house stick five pasties in the mike. I want to get off by half one. Don't want to miss John Gently, do we, Gwen?"

"Oh no," cackled Gwen into the cauliflowers. "Not John Gently. Can't miss that now, can us?"

There was nothing I could do. We were going to see Howard "The Defender" Powell open the Spring Fete. And Pinny's yellow flowers would be split and sold by the pumps, at ten for 60p. But I could look, and I could listen; and if I couldn't bring her daffodils, I could, perhaps, bring Pinny Cletchley Fete.

I looked in Howard Powell's eyes and I liked them.

"Who's it to?" he asked.

"Mrs Pinder – Pinny," I said. "Can you make it out to P–I–N–N–Y, please."

"Friend of yours?"

"She's an old lady in the old folks' home where I go and see my Uncle Champion. She doesn't get out much, so I tell her things I do and bring her stuff sometimes."

Howard Powell bent his head. He wasn't baldie on top at all. He had thick silver hair and a head like a football. He wrote: "To Pinny, best wishes, Howard Powell", smoothing the carrier bag as he wrote. It was all I had for him to autograph. He pushed it over. His handwriting was clear and careful, as though he'd taken trouble.

The sides of the tent sucked in and out as the wind walloped through. It was a bit like sitting in a giant lung. The queue for autographs coughed and quacked outside, but Howard Powell was heavy over his table. He had shoulders like a bus. No one would hurry him.

He put out his chin and joined his hands like

a bank manager. His eyes were joky behind his brown-tint glasses. The ball's in your court, they said. The chicken drumstick's in your bucket. Luckily, I had a question. It was the same question I'd had in my head ever since his little speech to open the fete.

"*How* did he come to a sticky end – " I asked – "William Bowhays Johns?"

"Ah," said Howard Powell...

M and I had had a bit of trouble making the fete by two. *The Defenders* theme was crashing over the field already as we dodged the programme vendors by the gate. The stand by the hedge drew everyone across like iron filings to a magnet. In amongst everyone else I spotted Natalie Pearce, Sean Pike, Jamie Tree, Claire Hindle, Duncan Pengelly and Leanne Cox and her brother – and wished I hadn't.

Mrs Sleep was fighting a microphone on a stand draped in a Union Jack. Behind the stand they'd rigged an orange tent which cracked in the wind. "Autographs 50p" said the sign. The Union Jack filled and fell on the platform and the sky and the clouds tore down across the brilliant slopes beyond, all the way out to Cap Hill. The colours smacked you in the eye from way across the field: red, white and blue – the flag – and orange, blue and green – the tent, the sky, the fields, bright as a sunburst.

Mrs Sleep took up her papers. She huffed in the mike. The wind tore her scarf over her face and whipped away half of what she said:

"As Chairman of the Spring Fete Committee, I am especially ... to welcome a very special ... since his residence at Stopeley I'm sure we all ... kindly given up his time to come along today and ... someone I'm sure you all ... star of *King's Bluff* and *The Revengers*..."

A large overcoat stepped forward. It flapped its arms irritably. "*The Defenders, The Defenders*," it husked.

"I mean, of course, *The Defenders*," said Mrs Sleep, simpering all over the shop. "Star of *The Defenders* – Mr Howard Powell."

She stepped down, having made a mix-up of the only thing she had to do, silly old bird.

Howard Powell gripped the microphone. He looked as broad as he was tall from where I stood. The tail of his classy overcoat clapped behind him in the wind. The sun flashed off his glasses. Everyone waited to see how he'd carry it off.

"Looks like he's in television, dun't he?" hissed M. "You can tell."

"Delightful," he was saying against the wind. "Delightful to be called to perform this ... here in Cornwall once more ... so many happy memories. In sixty-four Camilla and I had the pleasure ... on location in Newquay. I think I may safely ... of calling myself a native, returning, as I do, to distant Cornish roots ...

and in taking Stopeley I hope to ... escape the fate of a previous owner, one William Bowhays Johns ... who came, I understand, to a rather sticky end..."

He half turned to Mrs Sleep. She smiled round brightly as if he'd made a brilliant joke or something. The Spring Fete Committee behind her smiled and laughed a bit just to be on the safe side.

Howard Powell gave everyone his big smile. "May I say how much it ... this welcome return. I hope you will all ... this *plethora* of stalls. I now declare ... well and truly *open*. Thank you."

The autographs tent lumped and walloped against its pegs. Howard Powell waited. Perhaps he was remembering his speech, like me.

"*How* did William Thingy Johns come to a sticky end?" I asked again.

"It seems he was shot. Shot dead whilst loading flowers on Morden Quay by a youth named Harry Start. Some dispute over land tenancy."

"Did they get him for it?"

"Harry Start? Tried at Exeter six weeks later."

He nodded sagely, like a judge. He held it just about a minute longer than anyone else would've done. I wasn't entirely sure of him. But he was very sure of himself.

Howard Powell was orangey-green. It

wasn't too surprising. Of course he'd look orange – he was an actor, wasn't he? An actor, acting a part. Right now, he was acting Famous Howard Powell Opens a Fete. But there was a trusty undertow of green about him I couldn't help liking a lot.

"An interesting man, William Bowhays Johns," he went on. "They used to call him the Flower King. Ever hear that? The Flower King?"

I shook my head. "I haven't, no."

"Well," said Howard Powell, "he lived at the turn of the century, so perhaps you wouldn't… Did you know it was William Bowhays Johns who brought daffodils to the Valley? And narcissus – and gentians, for the toffs. I have his journal at Stopeley. Every trip to Covent Garden, meticulously logged. Marvellous handwriting."

"Yours is OK, too," I said stupidly. "Not bad for a quick job on a carrier bag."

It was a dozy thing to say, I don't know why I said it. Then I got hitched round the table-leg when I got up to go. I almost fell on the grass and dragged the table with me. The fact was, from the minute he'd started up with the Flower King stuff, I'd had such a stab of yellow in the guts I just wanted out, out of that heaving lung-tent and into the fresh air.

"Mind how you go," said Howard Powell kindly. The tent flap flopped. I was out.

"Take your time, why don't you?" said a big woman next in line. She snapped her autograph book. "Who are you – Wogan?"

But what got me was, when I finally got home and turned out the stuff I'd bought at the fete on the kitchen table, what really got me was, everything was yellow. The fireball gums, Super Soccersearch, hi-glo laces, joke book, maxiball, rollertorch, the transfers, stickers – everything. Everything I'd bought was yellow.

CHAPTER
THREE

Friday night I went up the paper shop by way of Mount Hope. One place I *wasn't* going was the daffodil field.

I'd been picking for M in the flower field every night since Sunday. The daffs had gone so well by the pumps, she wanted a bucketful every day after school. And what did I get out of it? I got to miss Club on Wednesday and drag off up the newsagent Friday, as *well* as picking, thank *you* very much.

Mount Hope lay left on the long steep lane to Top Road. It was nothing special to look at – two cottages, one done up, one not. Lower Hope, with the UPVC windows and the flat roof extension, was Sean Pike's house. The other was, had been, Pinny's.

It was a squashed little cottage, untouched for years. The mystery was, no one had snapped it up along with the adjoining field and done a number on it. Mount Hope itself had missed out on plastic windows, and I was glad. I pushed in the gate and scuffed round the overgrown garden. Pinny would have liked to have seen it. Or maybe she wouldn't. Maybe she wouldn't have liked to have seen her father's garden tangled over and lost. "A proper gardenin' man," she'd said. Better not, perhaps.

It was "Mount Hope", always "Mount Hope" with Pinny. Mount Hope, where she'd lived all her life till the day she married into Chubb's Row in Downlake, Mount Hope she'd talk your back end off about, given a whisker of a chance.

Everything in Pinny's life rolled home to Mount Hope. Here the Hand family had lived, all eight of them, high on the ridge that held up Top Road and peaked to Cap Hill beyond. The view from the garden took in everything else that had mattered to her: the village with its mine-stacks; the Valley, fluffy with tree-tops; the lazy slowboat river; the moors to either side. "A place to ourselves", Pinny had called it. It was all of that and more.

The fowl-house, or chicken shed, she remembered, was nothing but a beaten old lean-to down on its knees. Some capers they'd had, some capers, with the pig in the fowl-house. Sometimes the *chicks* would drop down, then the pig that lived below would eat them. Yuk.

There was something in the ground by the fowl-house door. I picked it up. A rusty half-moon. I turned it over. Four nail-holes, to nail it snug to – to what? It was something like a horseshoe, yet nothing big enough for any horse I'd ever seen. A horseshoe, but not a horseshoe, by a fowl-house that was a pig-house, on Mount Hope, which hadn't any hope at all. No hope of comfort, anyway, inside.

The room through the window was dark as a bag. I could just about make out dim strips of wallpaper trailing down between the beams, a fireplace choked in muck – and that was that. A single, choked-up room – for eight. Of course, there was the kitchen lean-to on the side; but upstairs this same room-space would be halved again, for bedrooms...

Suddenly the end lean-to window cracked open. My heart jumped up like a rocket.

"You comin' in, or what?" said the window. Somehow, for some reason, it was Sean Pike's sister. Sonia Pike, in Pinny's house.

"You just about gave me a heart attack, you did."

"Shouldn't go stickin' your nose in then, should you?" She hitched up the window and stuck out an arm. "Through here. It's easy."

It wasn't easy at all. By the time I stood up

in the kitchen lean-to I was all over muck and old paint.

Sonia Pike grinned. I'd never liked her. "Don't go much on climbin', do you?"

"I don't go much on breaking in," I said, like a nerd.

"Why d' you do it, then?"

"Why do you?"

She shrugged. "I always do. Me an' Sean mucks around in here sometimes."

There wasn't a lot to see in the dark and damp. Pinny's mother's Cornish range hung open in the end wall like a broken mouth, choked in chimney dust, twigs and soot. Smack on the hot-plate, where once Pinny's dinners had sizzled, sat a musty fat bird's nest, black as the range.

"Bird's-nest soup for tea," I said weakly. And then: "I know about this range."

I tried to latch the oven door, lifting and pushing at the same time, but even so, it wouldn't go. It weighed half a ton. Inside, it was dark as a coal hole, except there, at the back – blackened stonework and a ragged hole. The back of the oven had broken away. I could see clear through to the cottage wall behind.

"What *do* you know, then?" Sonia Pike asked snottily.

"I know more'n you," I said, pushing my face in hers. "I know Mrs Pinder, who's lived here twenty years. And I knew the back of the range was broken out before I looked, because she told me."

Sonia Pike backed off. "So?"

"She told me they used to have to go out and get these, what she calls tobs, from the garden – like turf – and lay it down the back here – " I waggled my arm behind the range – "between the back of the oven and the wall, to keep the heat in. Else he wouldn't cook at all."

"So?"

I looked at Sonia Pike. Could *anyone* like her?

"So, it was their landlord let them live in a tip with the range half bust, and never did a stroke on the place. Bowhays Johns was hard as nails," I finished, quoting Pinny, "and he never did nothing at all."

Bowhays Johns. Not your average, everyday name. That's why I'd pricked up my ears at the fete. That's why I'd asked Howard Powell. Whenever Pinny told life at Mount Hope, the landlord's name was never far behind. She didn't know how they'd stuck it, now. It seemed to me that Bowhays Johns, the Flower King, may have got what he deserved from Harry Start on Morden Quay. As landlord of Mount Hope and half the land around, he'd been no friend to Pinny.

Sonia Pike shrugged. What did *she* care about hard landlords and broken ranges? Suddenly she kicked the firebox door. Smaller than the oven door, it swung wide heavily. Deep across the firebox floor lay mini-horse-shoes in a rusty pile, like the one I'd picked up in the garden.

"Seen these?"

"Yeh," I said. "What are they?"

"Dunno. There's tons around out back. I got thirty-two in there."

She clapped the firebox shut with her foot. She looked around for something else.

"Want to do ripping? Me an' Sean do ripping."

Catching a tag of wallpaper left of the range, she stripped it the length of the wall.

"Don't," I said hotly. "Leave it alone."

"Not *your* place, is it?"

"Not yours either. People lived here and did stuff once, so – so leave it go."

What did I care about the wallpaper? The fact was, I *did* care. The fact was, I wanted Sonia Pike out, because she didn't feel the same way about Mount Hope I did. Perhaps if I went, she would too.

"I'm going," I said. "I got to catch the paper shop."

She said something, I don't know what. I forced out through the window and dusted off the damage on the other side.

"Why're you nosin', anyway?" asked Sonia Pike through the window. "That drippy artist was nosin' here Wednesday, as well. That Margaret Bath."

Now *that* was interesting. That was the best thing she'd said since she opened the lean-to window. Margaret Bath at Mount Hope – why?

I turned for a parting shot.

"You know what *you* are, don't you?" I said. "You're *purple*, that's what *you* are."

It was the worst colour I could think of. The worst thing I could think of to call her I could be sure she would never understand.

I woke at four in the morning, I don't know why. But straight away, the evening at Mount Hope came back. I ditched a pillow and humphed around, but back it came again, wild and crazy pictures flashing by like trains. The view over the valley; the window cracking open; Sonia Pike's arm coming out; flakes of paint on my sleeve; bits of wallpaper; the musty bird's nest; Sonia Pike's face. Sonia Pike, like a damp frog on my forehead that wouldn't go away. My hand on the gate that said "Mount Hope"; the fowl-house door; the range again, this time decked in daffodils, choked with them, the firebox overflowing yellow over the murky floor. I sat up. Yellow. It was Saturday again. There was something I had to do.

Outside, it was barely light. I would go now

– why not? The flower pickers had. They were out in the fields by five, bending their backs as the dawn rose. And flower picking was what I had in mind.

I put on the stuff I'd worn the night before and let myself out across the road and down the lane. Nothing could have been easier. I passed the filling station, closed for once, its pumps covered and its till dead. The sky was lightening every moment, the air had a special edge. By the time I came up Jago's Cross I was sharp as a razor, all alone in the new morning air, with the hassly day ahead two cool hours away. This was *my* time.

"Mee–oo." I saw them as I took the corner. "Mee–oo." They were high in a hold-pattern, waiting for updraughts, for the land to warm in the sun. The gate was heavy and wet; but the field lay before me, crisp as a sheet. This time, I would be more selective. This time I would pick and choose.

I checked the labels at the bottom of every row. My back warmed slowly as the sky picked up some heat. I read the names of every variety, even the deadheads on blasted stalks.

Golden Triumph was the main cropper, the thick yellow block of market blooms. But further over the hill lay stripes of a different colour. The pearly-whites – ivory trumpets and petals – were labelled Sonata. Then came Mohr's Bugle – orange trumpets, yellow petals; Sweet Success – a smaller white; Madame D'Or – large yellow; Lawry's Golden Belle – a whopper with frilly skirts; Lady Marjorie – small orange trumpet, off-white petals; Pot o' Gold – a dense yellow double.

And the narcissus: Harvest Moon – pale and papery; Humboldt's Goldeneye – classic orange and white; Mary Owen – delicate green-veined white; Pride o' the Valley – larger, creamier. And Little Addie – smallest of all. I liked Little Addie a lot. It wasn't puffy or over-bred. It didn't shout. That was why I liked it.

So many names, so many paintbox yellows. Which to choose? I spent a long time choosing, I don't know how long. How had the flower pickers bent for hours? The sun was breaking behind the oak on the hedge, orange as the heart of Little Addie, when I stopped to peel off my sweater.

In the end I made Little Addie my centre-piece. I thought it stole the show with its crinkly white heads, so papery-thin you could see your hand through them. Around them I made a thick ring of mixed Madame D'Or and Pot o' Gold – for the yellowness of them – together with some ivory Sweet Success for contrast.

Now the field was steaming like a kettle, steaming off its overnight dew as the big fat sun broke like an egg over the sky. I stood in the warm wet mist a long time, faffing about with daffodil leaves. A few leaves would bring out the colours.

I checked my watch. Seven-ten already. The video returns wouldn't sort themselves. And there were shelves to stack. I would have to stop, but I could hardly tear myself away. A few more, just a few more – the gorgeous lines of all the sorts I hadn't picked tugged me to stay, though I had already more than I could hold. But M on a Saturday morning could be ugly at the best of times; if pushed for time, she'd rat on Needham's and Uncle Champion. She only went anyway because she thought she ought to.

Coming back along the lane I saw the store lights blazing, early risers filling commuter specials on the forecourt. My clean and lonely morning-time was over. But I had an appetite for breakfast I hadn't had in a long time. Somehow, I'd done what I was meant to do. The early sun hadn't smiled on me for nothing. Not for nothing, the armful of Valley flowers that squeaked against each other as I walked. I would sneak in round the back and hide them in the shed. Then I would chug down a mighty bowl of Cocoa Pops. Later, I'd put them in the carrier bag autographed by Howard Powell. And then I would be ready for Pinny.

CHAPTER
FOUR

Catherine Cuthburt stood on the main stair-case, red as a traffic light. I caught the panic off her like a laser beam from one end of the hall to the other as M and I rounded the porch door. I knew at once something was wrong.

"On her own head be it," said Catherine Cuthburt dramatically.

She was three steps up, stiff as a ramrod. Someone had pushed her panic button, and she was going to make the most of it. Two care assistants flashed across the hall, going in opposite directions.

Someone was making a phone call under the stairs. It sounded like Mrs Screech.

"About half an hour ago," Mrs Screech was saying, her voice sharp and anxious. "We didn't think for a moment she could ... a wheelchair, yes, so she can't have gone far. I've got two out looking now. But I thought I ought to report ... Needham's Green ... yes. On Chapel Street ... I will, if she does ... she's eighty-four ... Mrs Pinder ... if you would ... all right. Thank you."

"She doesn't know she's born," thundered Catherine Cuthburt from the stairs. "She's got a room of her own and she doesn't know she's born. But she'll soon find out – *out there*." She smiled loopily, lasering me several shades of pink.

M collared Mrs Screech. "What's on, then, Dot? Where's Mrs Pinder to?"

"If I knew, I wouldn't be ringing the authorities, would I?" snapped Mrs Screech. "She let herself out the front. Janet gave her milky coffee at ten-thirty. No one seen her since."

I closed my eyes and rolled it all round in my mind. Pinny had done a runner. It was amazing, delicious. At this very moment she might be freewheeling down Fore Street, flying down to the West End Fry with the wind in her hair. It was amazing she should even try. What the flub had made her do it?

Mrs Screech flapped off. I wasn't sorry. I turned to M and told her I'd go out and look for Pinny as well, if she'd go on up to Uncle Champion, but she didn't like it much.

I said, "I'm going out to look. You go on up."

"It's all on her own head," raved Catherine

Cuthburt. "She'll find out, soon enough…"

"Daft old bird," said M. She pushed past her on the stairs. "Get on down the day lounge dear, an' give it a rest, I should."

I stood by the gate, which said "Needham's Green" in faded green ironwork, thinking like a maniac. Somehow, I would be able to feel where she'd gone. If I couldn't, who could? Redmoor was only a small town. There were only so many places she *could* be. One thing was certain – she'd gone right, down the road. She could hardly have gone left up the slope to New Street in a wheelchair unless she'd arms like a weightlifter, which she hadn't. No, she'd trickled down the slope to – to where? Cumberbatch the Chemist, perhaps, for more lily of the valley talc? "The Jamboree", on Back Lane? The Jamboree Cafe, where half of Redmoor traded gossip through fag smoke thick as stink?

I started on down the road, faster as I neared the crossing, and faster yet on the other side. Suddenly I knew where Pinny had gone. The wonder was, how she hadn't gone under a bus on the way across the road.

I wasn't wrong. I could see her old bird's-nest head through the window, under the "Transfloral – Bloomin' Lovely" sticker. What took me so long? Of course, Pinny was in Esme's Florist.

I looked in. The bell on the door dinged. But

neither Pinny nor Esme looked up.

"No dear, tin't likely," Pinny was saying. "Tin't likely I'd want they freesias. If you got no narcissus I won't 'ave nothin', dear. But an't you got none up behind?"

"We don't do much in narcissus these days, Mrs Pinder. Not for bouquets. I can do you pinks or carnations—"

"Not at they fancy prices," snorted Pinny. "All I want's a bunch o' Valley daffs. I'm sure you got some in back, dear." She screwed up her eyes. "En't that they, there?"

"In the corner? No, that's Chinese lily." The florist looked up desperately. It wasn't Esme, after all. It was her daughter, Annette. "I've shown you all we have, Mrs Pinder. Perhaps you'd better—"

"It's all right," I said, taking the handles of Pinny's wheelchair firmly. Somehow, I still had my bag of flowers. I plopped them in her lap. "Pinny, look. I picked 'em myself. This morning."

She craned around in her chair. Her face lit up like a beacon. She pushed my arm, as old friends do.

"I might've knowed – I might've knowed 'twas you. Well, now – " she gathered up her flowers. "Did you ever?"

"Thanks anyway," I told Annette. "Mrs Pinder's got to go now."

"Just so she's got what she wants," said

Annette, slightly cheesed.

It was lucky Annette *hadn't* had what she'd wanted, since Pinny never carried money. Mrs Screech had held it in hand since she'd last lost her purse.

It was lucky, too, there was no step to lug her chair over. I swung her out and away up Church Row, counting myself lucky to have caught her when I did. From Church Row we could cut left on Back Lane – and so up to Needham's again. She was pretty heavy to push. It was a bit like pushing a supermarket trolley full of spuds with something caught in the wheels. I had my head down along Back Lane, giving it some welly, when I saw she was snuffling in her flowers.

"All right? Pinny? All right?"

But she wasn't all right at all. She was way down in her daffodils, all messed and streaky. Her back shook gently. I couldn't – I couldn't hardly take her back up Needham's in a state. I'd have to give it a while, at least, whatever it was.

"Here we are," I said brightly, as though I'd planned it all along. "Here's the old Jamboree." It was a brainwave. I would buy her a cup of char in the cafe. That would set her right. "Want to nip in the old Jammie a minute?"

I knew this would be irresistible. How long was it since she'd last sat gassing over a cuppa up the Jammie? A very long time indeed, that was for sure. We biffed up over the single step with quite a bit of bother; but someone held open the door, and then we were in.

I slotted her in at the end table and asked her what she wanted.

"What you having? Fancy a bun? Hang on, I'll get you a cup of tea."

She looked up at last, all bleary. Her nose and cheeks were yellow with pollen, just like I'd pictured them when I first thought of daffodils. A warm feeling filled me up like syrup. This was something. However we'd got here, this was exactly right.

"Don't want no more tea," she said, something like the old Pinny again. "Get enough tea up Screech's." She always called Needham's "Screech's", after Mrs Screech. "I want one o' they fizzies. A fizzy an' a chocolate slice."

"We can't stop long, Pinny," I told her. "They're going spare up Needham's."

"Old Screech is wild, en't she?" She grinned wickedly at the thought. "Let 'un go. Her's got it comin'."

I told her I'd be back in a minute, and went to the counter. I got two Diet Sports and a chocolate slice. Then I ordered a big plate of chips. This would probably break the bank, but it was worth it.

Soon Pinny's mouth had a chocolate smile. When Johnnie Mace brought her the plate of chips he brought with him a red napkin over his arm. He set the table as though she were royalty, joshing her till she was pink and thoroughly scandalized. Several over by the corner sent her a nod and: "All right, Ad?" She loved every minute. I couldn't have chosen better if I'd tried. But there was something I wanted to ask her, and now was the time.

"You know the other Saturday," I began. "Saturday fortnight, when I was tellin' you about Rumbold's? Were you wanting – thinking about – daffodils, then?"

Her face, full of chips, quivered and broke. Why had I even tried? No wonder that yellow was so big and so clear. It was hitched up in a lot of – of what? What was it all about?

"I went up Cletchley Fete last week," I said hurriedly, to change the subject. "Seen the paper? Know who opened it? Look at the bag. The carrier bag your daffs're in."

She was too confused. In the end I had to haul out the bag from under the table and show her. "See? 'To Pinny, best wishes, Howard Powell'. You know, Howard Powell? *The Defenders*? I got that for you in the autograph tent."

Her eyes were misty, faraway. "'Tis very good o' you, dear. You're too good to me by 'alf."

I thought of telling her about the fete, but I could see she wasn't in the mood. Then I remembered something else. I felt around in my pocket.

"What's this? D'you know?" I clonked the horseshoe-that-wasn't on the table, the rusty half-moon I'd found by the fowl-house door at Mount Hope.

It was the right move. She actually smiled. "Don't see they no more," she said. "'Tis scoots, dear. Scoots for nailie boots."

"What's scoots?"

"Scoots is, well, this here, on the heel. When your heels was wore down, you'd go off up Top Road with a pattern paper for scoots an' toe-caps. An' the man'd measure it out an' cut it. Then Father'd nail on they scoots by the back door."

"On your nailie boots? And rip off the old ones?"

"Several o' they in the choke up Mount Hope. Oh, yes. Several o' they."

"I know," I said carefully. "That's where I got it."

Suddenly she was lively as a cricket. "Mount Hope, oh, yes, I bin thinkin' about Mount Hope. An' I been thinkin' about—"

"What? What have you been thinking about, Pinny?"

She looked all around. She flapped her hands on the table. She felt under it, blindly, for her flowers. I helped them into her arms.

"I been thinkin' about Mr William," she

said, her old eyes brimming tears. "Young Mr William, as got shot, years an' years back now. All them years gone by, since Mr William fell."

She cradled her flowers and shook. I finished the chips thoughtfully. What could I do? At last she looked up.

"I been thinkin' you must have knowed. You brought me Little Addie, you must have knowed. I been achin' all along for Little Addie and they yellow Valley flowers."

"Know what? Pinny, know what?"

"Oh, well now," she waggled her head, teasing. "Well now, say you don't know." She drew up the heads of her narcissus lovingly. "Who's Mr William namin' they for, but for me?"

"*You're* Little Addie? I just thought you'd like them, I never—"

"He said to me, Addie Hand, these is named for you. That's what Mr William said. I named 'em for you, Addie, an' your name's goin' to live on in the Valley a lot longer time than what mine is. That's what Mr William said when I was risin' nine, all them years ago. Up Stopeley, that was."

"Stopeley Rise? That's where Howard Powell—"

"Mother walked up Stopeley, yes, all along by Buttscombe Fields – that was in strawberries there, then. She'd walk up Stopeley, do the sheets an' all the washin' for Bowhays Johns, an' I'd peg along. Then we'd drag on 'ome.

I was only eight year old, an' I pegged along, all the way back up Mount Hope."

"And that's how you knew William Bowhays Johns that got shot?"

"I knew Mr William, yes, an' Mr William knew me, from pickin' as well, see? And Mr William, he was a lovely man, Mr William, he…"

I shook my head to clear it. She was swamping me deepest blue. Sorry, come-back-and-make-it-right-again blue, way down from the place where things done can never be done over.

"He'd come in the fields, see, he'd come in among the pickers and see 'twas done proper. And he'd see to bunching – I never was no good bunching. He used to say to me, 'Addie, put in a hand and come up twelve', that's what he used to tell me, an' I'd put in a hand and come up sixteen. Never was no good bunching. But he was a lovely man, Mr William…"

Deeper and deeper. Aching, so-sorry blue. What *was* it? What *was* it she was sorry for?

"What is it, Pinny?" I said. "What is it?"

She took a breath. She looked down, looked up again.

"There was one day, 'twas early in the fields, just comin' light, when Mr William walked by bottom 'edge. He got the orders, see? Special order o' Golden Belle for the boats that day, and he walked by bottom 'edge. An' I was

pickin', pickin' away those old yellow daffs –
only eight, and me back screamin' murder, but
carry on, pickin' an' pickin' an'—"

"And what? What, Pinny?"

"This dark boy come up behind. Tall boy.
I never seen him till he come up behind, and he
points and he says to me, is that man
Mr William? I says, yes, Mr William. Then he
says to me, all dark in his face, he says,
Mr William Bowhays Johns? An' I says, yes,
'tis Mr William. Then he asks me, where's he
to next, Mr Bowhays Johns? An' I tells him,
down to Quay. Down to Quay? says he, an' I
tell him Morden Quay, to make up orders.
Then he off an' rubs his face an' goes. An' I'm
pickin' an' pickin' a long time, and the sun's
up, and then –"

I waited for her to finish. She was too far
gone, now, not to.

"I'm pickin' in the yellow, the yellow Golden
Belle, and in the yellow I sees a man like in a
dream, a man kneelin' with flowers all around
and water in behind, and the man's Mr
William. Then directly I sees a young man walk
up an' draw a pistol. I see his dark face, an' his
eyes rollin' white, an' I see the pistol puff when
he goes *bang!* – and I see the blood fly out on
Mr William's waistcoat, an' I see his face
change, and him fall, fallin' back in the flowers. I see the young man drop the pistol and run
for dear life. But Mr William's dear life's spent

50

an' gone an' he's layin' in the daffodils for market. I shake me 'ead an' I see it all agin, an' the young man with the pistol's the one who asked me, is that man Mr William?"

She paused for breath. It was a long speech for Pinny.

"An' I felt meself poorly then. I din't know what to do, whether stop in the field with mother or fly to Quay. But then word come up directly, Mr William was killed down Morden. He was layin' dead in the Golden Belle, same as I saw it, exac'ly the same ... an' it was *me* told the dark face boy it was Mr William."

"It wasn't your fault," I told her softly. "How were you to know?"

"It was *me*, see?" Tears streamed down her face. "If I hadn've said nothin' he never would've got killed, see? It was *me* told the boy as shot him it was Mr William..."

This was worse than ever. But tears or no tears, I had to take her back. I gave her a minute or two with a tissue, then swung her wide of the table. Johnnie Mace held the door. He bowed her out like a queen. I told him, she'd be all right, she'd be fine, and off I pushed her, up Back Lane and away.

It was a lot harder than I thought. All the way up Chapel Street she told me she didn't want to go. The slope nearly killed me. I stopped halfway for a breather. I wasn't even sure I could *get* her up to Needham's, she was so dead-weight heavy in her chair. I could jam her by the wall and go for help; but I had a feeling she might trickle off again, and not mind the crossing at all, the way she was.

She craned around again. "Don't you mind me, bird," she said. "You go on 'ome, an' I'll stop here."

I shook my head. "You can't stop here. What will you do?"

She covered my hand with hers. "Take me up Mount Hope, then, dear. I been thinkin' so much on the old place latterly. Won't you take me up 'ome?"

It was truly pathetic. What could I do? But it all made sense to me now – even the yellow. Especially the yellow. The colour of Golden Belle that Mr William fell in, the colour of hope.

"Listen," I said. "You go back up Needham's now – and I'll take you up Mount Hope."

"Up the old place? Shall you?"

"Sometime soon. I promise."

"Say when? Say promise when?"

"I can't promise when. But I *will*."

"Say promise."

"Promise."

It was good enough to put her quiet. *How* I was going to get Pinny to Mount Hope was something else again. All the way up the slope, I wished I hadn't said it.

I was completely naffed by the time the gate was in sight. We were dragging along one step at a time when a cool hand closed on mine. And another, taking the handles from me. I looked up. It was Margaret Bath. Margaret Bath the painter, tall and warm and brown. The same moment, M popped out of Needham's Green ahead. She waved like a semaphore signal.

Margaret Bath looked down like an angel. "Shall I take her now?"

It was a funny thing, but all the way home in the car I thought Howard Powell was following behind. It was an old cream Jag. The driver looked just like him. The sun flashed off his glasses. It was – wasn't it?

Coming along Top Road, he overtook. I almost waved – I did wave – but it was someone else entirely. The face behind the glasses was wrong. I don't know why I thought it was him. Why should I have Howard Powell on the brain?

I settled back in my seat, but I wasn't settled at all. One thing puzzled me, and that was William Bowhays Johns. If he'd been so fond of Pinny, why did he squeeze them for rent at Mount Hope? *How* was Mr William a 'lovely man' when he never did nothing at all on the place? It didn't add up. But then, those were the days when you took what you were given, and were grateful.

"Cheer up," said M. "It might never happen."

I forced a smile. What did I have to worry about? I only had to get an old lady, in a wheelchair, out of an old folks' home they'd never let her stir from again, three miles down the road to a squashed old cottage full of muck, and back again. That was all.

CHAPTER
FIVE

What happened next was Janie Powell. It happened this way. The Coalyards were five down to the Portables with ten minutes lunch hour on the clock, when Howard Powell pulled onto the forecourt in a silver BMW.

The Coalyard boys and the Pollock's Portable Buildings boys play volleyball over the wire netting most lunch times. Sometimes they'd rotate places like you're supposed to; more often Jez and Barf would be always opposite each other at the net, so's they could smack each other down on the high balls.

The wire netting which separates the top of our car park from Pollock's is too high for a proper net, anyway. It was coarse volleyball they played – sometimes too coarse. It got a bit abusive, sometimes. 'Specially Jez and Barf. Sometimes D would come out red in the face and tell them, knock it off. But then, D's got a pretty short fuse. Did I say? Well, I'm saying now. A pretty short fuse.

Anyway, it was around one-twenty. I was hanging out, watching, as usual. It was the second day of the Easter holidays; there wasn't a lot else to do. I could've slipped off down Paul Doney's – my mate Paul Doney's a good laugh – but I didn't. Too hot. Too far. *And* he'd be off out, probably. As it was, I was on the wall watching the Coalyards.

The Coalyards play from our side of the wire. They'd filter down from Furzeland Fuels and Plant Hire around half-twelve, buy lunch, then play. Sometimes I'd fetch the ball for them, when they lost it, which wasn't often. Mostly I'd just watch. It was better than being up the house with M.

I remember I was finishing an ice-cream Zone Bar when the silver BMW powered in. It died smoothly beside the lead-free. Jez had just spiked down a killer fifth for the Portables. But Barf let the ball zing up again past his ear. His jaw dropped. "Wow," he said. "Get *that!*"

The sleek shell cracked open. Howard Powell – it *was* Howard Powell this time – snapped cleanly out. He whipped off the petrol cap. He slotted in the fuel gun. He was surprisingly snappy for a man who looked like a circus tent. He didn't bother checking the counter on the fuel pump like most people, trying to stop it on five or ten quid's worth exactly. Instead he looked around. He had on a big shirt with pastel stripes and a pratty-looking scarf at the neck. He saw me over on the wall – he waved! Pretty nice, seeing he probably didn't remember who I was. I waved back. Then I sneaked in at the side door.

Gwen was on the till. In fact she was on the skive. She stuffed her magazine under the counter when she saw me coming. Then she checked the petrol register. The amount came through automatically from the pumps.

"Last of the big spenders," she said sourly, entering the total on the till.

"Yeh," I said, enjoying myself a lot. "It's Howard Powell."

"It never..." Gwen did a double take through the plate glass. "It's *him*! Oh, 'ang!"

I picked up a thrilling shade of puce. I realized Gwen really thought he'd notice her. Gwen was pretty old, at least as old as Howard Powell. She had dyed, ratty hair, a backside like a settee and a pug face. But still she thought – she actually thought – there was a chance Howard Powell would whisk her from Dawe's to a life of glamour. *It's possible, isn't it?* said Gwen's wandering left eye. *Well – isn't it?*

Suddenly I felt a shot of sympathy for Howard Powell. That was what everyone thought when they met someone famous.

Deep in their secret purple hearts, everyone thought a celebrity would see how they stood out from the crowd, how special they were, how like them.

The door opened. Gwen adjusted her eyes so they both looked in the same direction. A thin girl with square brown hair walked in.

She turned. "Dad. Mind the step."

Howard Powell followed her in. He looked around blankly. He held his chin, remembering something. "Yes," he said at last. "I know."

"Over here," said the girl, from the next aisle. "They haven't got gourmet. Too much to hope."

It seemed weird Howard Powell had a daughter, I don't know why. She wore strange beige culottes with braces over a black T-shirt with white writing on it. The writing was French. She wore a camera over one shoulder, a black rucksack over the other.

"Gourmet what?" I whispered to Gwen.

"Looks like he's in television, dun't he?" she hissed back madly. "You can tell."

We waited to see what they'd buy. The very best of it was, M was up the house reading the local rag over a corned-beef sandwich. This was the moment she'd been waiting for – and she was up the house, missing it. It wasn't lost on Gwen. We exchanged a look. Or it seemed to me we did. You could never be sure with Gwen.

Outside, the Coalyard boys were giving the BMW the once-over. They looked in the tinted windows. They hooted over the "HP1" reg. I hoped Howard Powell had the keys in his pocket. They were a bit spur of the moment, the Coalyards.

Howard Powell's daughter pulled out a trolley. She whisked it away down the aisle. Her helmet hair never moved an inch, she held her head so high.

Gwen and I heard cans going in, lots of them. Then up they came quickly to the off-licence section. Howard Powell put in a bottle of whisky. Then he put in a bottle of red wine. The girl took it out again. She shook her head disapprovingly. "Really, Dad." She picked out a different wine and showed him.

He nodded, smiling. "Find me a white that's not too grim, will you, darling?"

At last they wheeled up their trolley. Gwen was all of a fluff. She rang up the whisky twice by mistake. Howard Powell held up his hand and said he'd have another bottle, then they wouldn't fall out, would they? Gwen flushed up red and pleased. She didn't know what to say. Then she rang up the cans. There were twenty-eight, all dog food, the most expensive brands we carry. Gourmet dog food, that's what they'd been after. What were they going to do – eat it themselves?

Howard Powell nodded to me pleasantly.

"Autograph go down well?"

"Yeh, thanks," I said. "I took her daffodils, too." He really remembered. I was amazed.

He nodded again. "Daffodils. Can't go wrong."

Gwen was shelling out carrier bags like a madman. "Fifty-six, seventy-five," she said unsteadily. "Please."

"Haven't you got any boxes?" asked Howard Powell's daughter. "We don't take bags that aren't biodegradable, do we?"

"Absolutely not." He gave her a sappy smile. "Janie's down for the holidays, so we have to mind our *p*s and *q*s."

He pushed three twenties over the counter. "You might like to choose a video sometime, darling."

"I shouldn't think," she said. "We only like French directors, don't we?"

I went quickly through the boxes by the door, found two with the bottoms still in, and started packing away the dog food, right by Janie Powell's elbow. She didn't help at all. And all I could think of while I did it was what Pinny had told me about the Flower King and the day he died. I knew Howard Powell would want to know. It was on the tip of my tongue to tell him about it, but I didn't know how. I didn't even know if I should.

Then Gwen said something so stupid it drove away everything else.

"You'd never believe it," she said, "but years ago I was the spit of Rhetta Zest. Mother used to say, you got a look of Rhetta Zest on *The Defenders* with your hair up, Gwennie. Course, that was years back, now."

The worst of it was, she meant it. I looked at Janie Powell. I could see in her eyes Gwen might've come direct from the Planet Zog. Looking at them, it was hard to believe they were in the same universe.

Howard Powell leaned gallantly towards Gwen. "We saw Camilla at Cannes last year, didn't we, Janie? She looks very like you." He straightened. "Now," he added, in an undertone. I think I was the only one who caught it.

"Oh, come *on*, Dad," said Janie Powell coldly. "Hurry up."

I followed them out to the car with the second box and helped Howard Powell lump it in. While he faffed around in the boot I wanted to say: Did you know my friend Pinny knew the Flower King? Well, she did, and she pointed him out to Harry Start. Then she thought she saw him being shot in a funny dream. Then he *was* shot, and then she knew what she'd done. But she didn't know what was going to happen, she was only eight. Now she's really, really old, and she wants to be forgiven before she – she wants to be forgiven.

I wanted to say it so much, I thought the words would pop out on their own. But they didn't. I wanted to tell him I'd promised to take Pinny to Mount Hope and I didn't know how I was going to do it – but I didn't. I watched him stow the boot full, and I didn't say anything at all. And then the moment passed when I could have, and he was in the car beside pain-in-the-bum Janie. With a wave, he gunned the engine. And then he was gone.

The sun beat down on the stupid white concrete. Even the sight of M coming down from the house too late for anything didn't make me feel as good as it should have.

I left her rowing with Gwen over the till. "Well, why *din'* you? You could've rung up the house. Well, what'd he *say*? You could've shouted me. I've only been sat on me backside up the house. Did he, then? What'd he buy?"

"Booze and dog food," I shouted from the second aisle. "And petrol."

There was a camera in the middle of the bottom pet food shelf. Right between the cans, middle bottom shelf. I picked it up. I clicked open the case. It looked expensive. Inside the top of the camera case was a name, white on black. "J.P. Powell", it said. "Oakleigh School For Performing Arts". I clicked it shut again. I looked up. No one had noticed. I smirked at the dogs on the dog food cans, and the dogs on the dog food cans smirked right back. I tucked the camera under my sweater.

I'd always wanted to go up Stopeley Rise. The big house in the tall stand of trees by the river had always fascinated me. Suddenly I felt like a corned-beef sandwich, and I don't even like corned-beef.

CHAPTER
SIX

Through the stone ball gateposts and into the cucumber green. It was a rich man's drive, everything said so. And what I liked best about it was, there was no end in sight through the trees ahead.

The same breeze lifted my hair that had lifted the Flower King's coat-tails. The same sun shone down on me that had shone on the Flower King's coach-and-four. The trees were the same trees, the stones the same stones, that saw him pass by.

Not *just* the same, perhaps. Those trees had grown seventy-odd years bigger since the Flower King had lived at Stopeley Rise. They were lovely tall whispering beeches, more than a hug around. They'd have been a lot thinner, then. Perhaps Mr William had planted them himself. Or perhaps they were older still.

Anyway, they made a cool-cucumber world so different to the lowlife road outside that I felt like a thief in a church walking under them. I checked the camera in my pocket. I was returning something of value to the daughter of the house, wasn't I? No need to feel like a fart in an art gallery. But all the same, I did.

Around the bend the drive ran up to a pair of dull grey gates. I looked in. A cobbled yard, low grey buildings and a grim grey clock tower with a weather-vane. Stopeley wasn't so grand, after all. Where were the cool white walls that flashed in the trees from the road?

Then I realized. The doors all around weren't made for Flower Kings or other men, they were made for horses. This was only the stable yard, and these, the stables and coach house. I stepped down, impressed. The drive ran on beneath. It was a rich man's drive long enough to keep the world away. But at last it widened, and the trees fell away. I was coming up on Stopeley House itself.

Now then. I pulled out the camera. I ran through what I was going to say. Knock. Smile. "Hello. You left this up Dawe's the other day. Thought you might want it back."

I would have to spin it out a bit or they'd turn me off like a tinker before I had a foot in the door. An expensive camera was worth at least a glimpse in the Flower King's house – if only a look in the wash-house door, where

Pinny's mother had burst her hands boiling sheets in the copper.

It was a nice camera. For the first time I thought about what it would be like to keep it. I hadn't thought before, but I thought about it now, just when I was going to give it back.

The house was a thick cream house, not white at all. The front faced out across the valley. There wasn't a single other house in sight. Cletchley village could have been miles away, instead of under the hill. Stopeley House looked out on the steep river bank opposite with its woods tumbling down on the river, and on all the gorgeous runaway hills beyond.

There were two wings to the house, with a big front door between. The front door and the other doors and the windows and the gutters and the bargeboards were all painted a funny colour green. Not green, not blue – but something in between. There was a coat of arms over the front door. Two hawks with stately wings, pushing a badge between them. Hawks again. Mee–oo.

I was just going to knock when I noticed a bell-push job in the wall. The windows looked dark, the furniture inside darker still. I looked back up the cool drive. I could still run back up that long cool drive, if I wanted.

As soon as I pressed the bell an enormous row blew up inside, a deep-voiced dog barking and belling in some echoey hall. I could hear its claws scrabbling on the floor inside. The door shook. There was a pretty big dog on one side of that door, and me on the other. I was quite keen to keep it that way. Then I heard footsteps, a woman's voice, the dogs wolfing away down a passage.

The door opened. A tanned woman in beige and white looked out. "Yes?"

I smiled. I held out the camera. "Hello. Janie left this up Dawe's yesterday. Up the filling station."

She came out a little and took the camera. She didn't even smile. Through the gap in the door I could make out dim old flock wallpaper, a fancy mirror, a couple of paintings in gold frames, a small table with flowers. Somewhere deep in the house I could still hear the dogs.

"Is Janie in?"

"I think not," she said. "Thank you."

And she closed the door. And that was that. She hadn't really looked at me at all. She hadn't understood what I was asking. She hadn't wanted to. I looked at the door. I looked at the dull windows, at the door again. It was a bit like queueing for a film and having the "House Full" barrier cut me off at the ticket booth. I had handled it all wrong. I should have asked for Howard Powell. Howard Powell would have invited me in.

I started back up the drive like a burst

balloon, wondering why I'd ever come down it with any thrill at all. So much for seeing Stopeley at last.

I'd almost reached the old stables when I spotted Janie Powell. She was coming up some ornamental steps from a lower lawn. She saw me – and still she came on. She hopped up on the dim path. *"Bonjour,"* she said, coolly. Somehow it didn't sound pratty, the way she said it.

"I just came round to bring your camera back. You left it up the filling station. Yesterday."

She didn't answer straight away. First, she decided whether she wanted to or not.

"How boring of me," she said at last. Then: "I'm going in. Come if you want."

After a minute I followed her down the little flight of quartz steps and onto a smooth wide green. It broke, half a Wembley away, against the side of the house, in a flare of japonica. She walked across, and on through a rockery. She looked round once, to check I was following.

We slipped down, by a lawn still lower. She pointed through the bushes. "Look. Father in full flow. Quite diverting, really."

Quite diverting. I looked where she pointed. But first, I heard him. Howard Powell had his back to us. It was a broad back, in a silky purple dressing-gown. Underneath he had purple pyjamas. He was going through some routine, all by himself in the garden. His hair looked as though it had had a rough night. He turned sideways a bit. He was directing a stream of something over the bushes. For a moment I thought ... then I saw the hose. He had his thumb in the end of it, splicing the water into a high-pressure jet. He was watering the garden, sort of.

"My dear fellow," he told a large shrub, "you *might* threaten London, were you able to use the full power of the Rectifier –"

"John Gently again," whispered Janie Powell. "He always does *The Defenders* for a hangover."

"I'll trouble you to keep your hands in the air, sir," he warned the shrub, gunning it with his hose. "Your friends have been, ah, shall we say – detained?"

Suddenly he choked the water into a vicious needle. He brought the hose onto a mouldering old greenhouse in the corner. The water-needle drummed on the old glass roof. Several panes were missing already. The red brick walls beneath had lost most of their mortar. Howard Powell drilled his hose along the panes of glass.

Suddenly one of the panes popped out. The water piled in through the hole, slashing and bashing the inside wall of the greenhouse, fizzing in over the old crocks and pots, dry as dead men's bones. Howard Powell smiled. He was still John Gently. He slashed the water to and fro.

"My dear chap, you must choose your friends more carefully. And now, I must insist. The Rectifier, if you please."

"I wish he wouldn't *do* that," I whispered hotly. "That might've been the Flower King's greenhouse."

"It was," said Janie. "Four more on the other side of the wall. If you like all that Flower King stuff, I'll show you something. If it's not *too* boring."

"No," I said. "It's not."

As we walked to the house, I said, "Who was it who answered the door a minute ago?"

"Oh. Mrs Teagarden. She housekeeps for my father when I'm not around to look after him. Except she reads magazines most of the time."

"Where's your mum, then?"

"Aix en Provence. I'm spending August there."

A father and a Mrs Teagarden here. And a mother in France. And a boarding school somewhere else again. I couldn't imagine all the places she must have been. The furthest I'd ever been was Rumbold's Funpark, down West. And *that* was only because D had fancied a run to the monster Cash and Carry a stone's throw from Rumbold's. He wasn't about to put himself out to take me anywhere.

Not D. What would be in it for him?

We left Howard Powell ranting on the lawn, and we took the gravel path. At last we popped up by the big japonica at the side of the house. We passed by dim french windows with dimmer furniture behind. We came to a blue-green door. We went in.

The slate-flagged passage led left to a kitchen. No comfort here – this was servants' domain. Ahead and to the right lay panelled double doors. Janie Powell spread the doors ahead and listened. I listened, too. What were we listening *for*?

The ceiling was high, the carpets rich. We were in the hall I'd glimpsed not ten minutes before, on the other side of the front door that had shut me out so finally. Ha. I was in – no thanks to Mrs Teagarden. We crossed the hall like spies, past a broad flight of stairs. The brass stair-rods shone all the way up on the wine-red carpet. The old flock wallpaper had been wine-red too, once. Now it was bloody-brown. At the foot of the stairs stood a spindly little table, the sort that fell over if you breathed on it. It held a big china bowl of flowers of every colour.

Janie Powell opened the door on a deep and gloomy room. The walls, the fireplace, the furniture, the carpet and the curtains – all were deepest bottle-green.

"This room's called William's Kennel, I

don't know why," said Janie Powell. "It's on all the old plans of the house. Spooky, isn't it?"

I liked Mr William less already. So gloomy, so self-important – so bottle-green.

"Here's the Flower King," she said. "*If* you want to see him."

And there he was. The Flower King in an oval frame, dated eighteen ninety-nine, in the corner. He had a smooth face and a shiny nose. Shiny forehead, too. I don't know why they painted him that way. He looked as if he'd just sat down from a brisk walk. Maybe he had. A walk to the flower fields, perhaps. Or round his glasshouses and back. The Flower King looked out of his oval frame at me as though he was about to tell me something. "Top hole, old thing," probably. He looked a bit like that.

He didn't look that old. His light-brown moustache and beard were neatly trimmed. Twenty-something, I'd guess. He leaned forward in a dinner jacket with his right hand just showing above the edge of the frame. Between his finger and thumb he held a single white flower. It looked like a camellia. His cheeks were pink, as though he spent a lot of time outdoors. But he'd smarmed down his hair for the artist. Oh, yes, and put on his dinner suit and white bow-tie. He was a Bowhays Johns, wasn't he?

But I liked him. His mouth was a bit hidden, but I could tell he was smiling. His eyes wouldn't have made sense if he wasn't. Anyway, he was, he was smiling. Not a big smile – a pleasant, "have another, old chap" kind of smile. That's why his eyes were bright. The lines beneath them showed he smiled a lot.

I looked in the Flower King's eye and I knew, in that moment, that Pinny had nothing to worry about. The feeling was light blue – and light blue was refuge from the storm. I'd never got a colour off a thing before. How much of what I picked up off other people came from inside my own head? But in that moment I knew, whatever the Flower King had or hadn't done, whatever Harry Start had done to *him*, I knew that the Flower King *was*, had been, at peace with himself. He had lived and he had died – suddenly. And that was how it had been for him. How would a picture of Harry Start feel? Now *that* would be something worth feeling.

"I like him," I said, "the Flower King. Don't you?"

"I suppose," shrugged Janie Powell. She nodded at a dark portrait a little further over. "That's Mr William. Gruesome, isn't he?"

"I thought *this* was Mr William," I said quickly. "Mr William, the Flower King."

"Mr William the *Younger*." She patted the dark portrait beside him. "This one's his father. William Bowhays the Elder."

There was something a bit … something a

bit uncovered here. Like finding something on the beach and pulling and pulling it out of the sand and finding it much bigger than you thought it was, *and* something horrible on the end. I couldn't describe it at all, the feeling I got when I saw there were *two* Mr Williams. Had – had Harry Start known there were two?

William the Elder looked a bit like Father Christmas. But he didn't look kindly at all. His mouth was a yellow used-looking line in his beard. His eyebrows almost hid his eyes. But not quite. They were black button eyes, keen with self-interest. I didn't like them at all.

His black coat blended in the background of the painting so it looked as though his head was floating with no body under it at all. As I looked, the darkness crowded in around his face. It seemed to stand out as though it had depth, until all that was left was his hoary old whiskers and eyebrows – and under them, his beetle-black eyes. The blackness around him rose up against me, I could feel it, and the button eyes burned. "Me," they said. "Me – William Bowhays Johns. I wrung the money from tenants to build this house. I stop at nothing to get what I want."

I stepped back. I looked at the two of them. Suddenly I knew one thing for sure.

"This William's Kennel – it was William the Elder's room, wasn't it?"

"Of course it was," said Janie Powell. "The

wallpaper's original. So is most of the furniture."

I knew, for what it was worth, that the Flower King could never have made this gloomy den. For him there would be light, and air. This room had the mark of a heavier hand. There was no mistaking whose Kennel it was.

"Want a Spa-Spring?"

"A what?"

"A mineral water. A Spa-Spring."

"No. Thanks. Is there anything else?"

"Tomato juice?"

"I mean, anything else to do with the Flower King? Is there – is there a picture somewhere of Harry Start? I mean, not a portrait, just a—"

But she'd whipped off out to fetch a drink. I heard her softly crossing the hall. I heard the click of the double doors beyond. I was alone in Black William's Kennel.

CHAPTER
SEVEN

I stood at the window and looked and thought. Black William's black eyes drilled in my back. What was I *doing* here, anyway? What did I want? What did I *really* want?

I looked out on the rolling lawns and the rolling hills beyond, and I didn't see anything at all. It was a bit of a crunch for me, that time alone in William's Kennel. I knew one thing for sure – I wanted more out of life than the filling station. M and D had never been too bothered about my schoolwork. They weren't too bothered if I nicked off altogether, so long as I was useful round the stores. It was because they'd never thought I'd do anything else but help run Dawe's, some day. It had never entered their heads I might do anything else. It hadn't really entered mine, till now.

I went back to look at the Flower King.

There he was with his white camellia, leaning out of his frame like a kindly uncle ready to tip me a fiver. I looked in his eyes. I looked at the flower he held between finger and thumb, at his eyes again. Eyes, flower – flower, eyes. What? What was it? "Find what you love," blew the answer, like a hotline from him to me. "Find what you love – and do it."

I went to the mirror. I looked in. What colour would I be? I looked, and I didn't much like what I saw. What else but foggy grey? I didn't know what I wanted. I was grey and woolly and all mixed up. I could go any way, or none. I could paint on any colour, or leave the canvas blank.

I went to William the Elder and I stood and I faced him out. What, then? What? "Get what you want," said his burning beetle eyes. "Look what I got. Get what you want – and keep it."

A long heavy time seemed to pass, I don't know how long. Then there was purple silk between the beetly eyes and mine, rippling purple dressing-gown where there'd been none before, and an iron-grey head with tousled hair, and flashing arms gripping, lifting, cross-ing, straightening. Black William was gone. Howard Powell had turned him to the wall.

I stared at the back of the portrait. It was surprisingly rough. I stared at the frayed brown edging, the remains of a torn label, the mountings for the chain that held it to the wall.

I couldn't stop staring.

Howard Powell saw I couldn't stop. He waggled his face in mine and boggled his eyes. Then he Welsh-combed his hair quickly with his fingers. A lovely grass-green light lingered around him.

"I wouldn't look at the old beggar too long," he said. "I've commissioned a landscape to replace him. I'd chuck the evil old cuss in the attic now if it didn't spoil the wall. See?"

He lifted the corner of the portrait. I saw. Underneath, the wallpaper was rich and dark. The rest of the wall had faded. But what fascinated me was the place where Howard Powell had gripped the frame to turn it. It was glowing green.

"No one's evil," I said, staring at the place. "Everyone's a paintbox."

"A paintbox?"

"Take black."

"Yes?"

"Black's not evil, black just sucks up everything else. It's the hole the other colours fall in when they've nowhere else to go. What's left isn't human. You see them sometimes, not very often. They go around, and they *look* like people, but they're not really human at all. Inside, they're black."

I shivered, saying it. I'd never said it, not even to myself. "I've seen four I can remember. Four, and a picture." I looked

Howard Powell full in the face. He had a strange expression. "Old William's black inside. And *you're* green," I finished. "Right now."

Howard Powell tilted his head. He pushed his rimless glasses further up on his nose. "Oh. I'm green, am I?"

"You're green."

"That's good?"

I nodded. "The best."

"And you are…?"

"Grey. I'm grey."

"Well – Graham," he said. "We have to thank you for Janie's camera. Don't we, Janie?"

Janie Powell stood watching in the doorway as if I were mad or dangerous or both. A big silky Afghan hound job sat beside her, watching too. Was it something I said? Just how long *had* I been locked in Black William's eye, anyway?

The Afghan shifted its floor-mop feet. It whined and dipped its head as though it wanted Howard Powell. But it was careful not to put a paw over the line from red to green where the hall carpet met William's Kennel.

Howard Powell brought his hands together in a great dry clap. "Brunch in the loggia, I think. Give me ten minutes."

When he reached the door he turned. "Green, you say?"

"And orange. Sometimes."

"Is orange good too?"

I shrugged. "It's not anything. It's – pretending."

"Ah," said Howard Powell. "I do a lot of that."

When we got outside, we were around the other side of the house, the side I hadn't seen. Running along above the top of the french windows was a low and shady roof. It ran all the way along that side of the house. The outside edge of the roof rested on pillars that were dead tree-trunks. They'd been left lumpy and gnarled deliberately. Around them curled tender vine leaves, snaking from a mother of vine stems in the corner. This was the loggia. Brunch in the loggia. With Margaret Bath – if only I'd known.

She was sitting with Mrs Teagarden at an oval table spread in white. She had on something long and blue, and her thick brown hair ran all the way down over the back of her wicker chair. She was talking, pointing something out. Mrs Teagarden was nodding, skating the toe of her tan shoe on the ... the whatever-it-was in a pattern over the floor, nodding again. I could see Mrs Teagarden wasn't listening. She was more interested in her shoe.

Margaret Bath looked up. "Well, hello."

"*This*," said Janie Powell, "is Graham." Meaning, a horror-show on legs that had made it through life so far, she didn't know how, but this was what it was called.

"It isn't," said Margaret Bath instantly. "Dawe's boy, isn't it? I thought you—"

"Funny floor," I said. "What's all the lumps? Wood or something?"

"Guess," said Margaret Bath.

The patterned floor ran the length of the loggia. It was something like cobbles, but the cobbles weren't stones. They were something like knobbly wood, but they didn't feel like wood; they felt more like shells – and each cobble had three knobbles to it, and all the knobbles lay the same way. Little regular shapes in dusty dry grey lines, up and down, like a mat that had grown itself out of the ground. Fussy little shapes – I had a feeling I knew what they were, but I couldn't quite get it. They were something someone had collected. They'd collected a lot, and they weren't shells, they were –

"Not bone, is it?"

Margaret Bath stooped. She wobbled a loose bit in the floor, where gaps showed in the pattern. She pulled on a cobble, and it seemed horrendously long and toothy when it came all the way out – although it was only a little bone about five or six centimetres long. It had been buried end on, so the only bit that showed was the knobbly head. Under every knobbly head was a shaft of bone. Every head *was* a bone – and all of them together made a gruesome floor that looked like anything but what it really was.

"Lambs' knuckles," said Margaret Bath. "Clever, isn't it?"

"Ghastly things," said Mrs Teagarden. "They ruin a good court shoe."

"They must've – they must've had a lot of lambs."

"Of course, in William the Elder's day they would have entertained in the grand style. I expect Cook was instructed to save them."

I remembered the last time I'd seen Margaret Bath, on Chapel Street, when her cool hand had rescued Pinny's chair. *And* I remembered she'd been poking around up Mount Hope. What was she doing at Stopeley Rise? How did she come to know Howard Powell? And why was she *everywhere* I was – with her shaggy-dog hair and her hippy-drip dresses and her long white artist's hands?

Brunch was a new one on me. What it was, was tiny little fishes fried crispy in flour or something. Whitebait, they said. Lots of little hot crispy fishes, in two baskets. And little tri-angles of brown bread and butter, and slices of lemon. It wasn't too bad. Howard Powell brought out the tea himself. He'd changed into spammy beige trousers and an enormous sweater with leather elbows.

For a while he talked perspective with Margaret Bath. They talked colourwashes, evening shade, and avoidance of service wiring to the house. At last it dawned on me. Margaret Bath was commissioned to paint Stopeley Rise. It was her landscape which would elbow Black William from his Kennel. When I looked, I could even make out her set-up under the parkland oaks, way over left, where the lawns rolled up to a border brimming with shrubs.

Janie Powell and Mrs Teagarden talked dogs. Then they talked horses and riding tack. I listened and ate cake. Mostly, I ate cake. When I dropped my knife and picked it up I noticed Howard Powell had his hand on Mrs Teagarden's knee under the table.

I took another slice of cake since no one else was about to. I wondered if M would notice I hadn't set out the bread orders before I came away. If Dolly Gillet missed out on her Friday white sliced *again* there'd be a row...

"Young Graham here tells me I'm green."

There again, there'd been several extra white sliced in the tray. And Laycock's had cancelled – that meant four extra white, two brown. So long as Dolly Gillet's order was held back, it would... Who was on today? Friday. Lorraine was on. It would be OK.

"Oh, very green," laughed Margaret Bath. "How does he mean?"

"You'll have to ask him that," said Howard Powell.

Now they were all looking. I swiped the cake crumbs off my mouth and wondered why I'd ever mentioned the colours at all. I'd gone on years and years and never spilt it; why spill it now? I looked at the fish heads on my plate. Everyone else seemed to have eaten theirs. The fish heads eyed me through their batter and waited.

"Well," I said slowly. "It's not exactly easy to explain."

"Very taken with the old devil's portrait in the Kennel," said Howard Powell in a faky whisper. "Had to be rescued, didn't he, Janie?"

Janie Powell rolled her eyes. "Psycho," she said.

"I hate that picture," put in Mrs Teagarden feelingly. "I snagged a Rivelli cashmere on the frame last week. The shoulder's out. Ruined."

"Harry Start – " I blurted – "Harry Start didn't mean to shoot young Mr William. I don't think."

Everyone looked. Then Howard Powell nodded. "Harry Start made no defence. Harry Start kept mum. Of course, there was speculation. I've got the newspaper cuttings."

"Well," said Margaret Bath. "I know the Start family lost the tenancy of their farm just before Harry came of age. But that was due to William the Elder."

"What happened?" I asked.

"Harry Start's father had farmed Start's Meadow all his life, and *his* father before him – but he died when Harry was twelve. A 'caretaker' tenant farmer was foisted on the family by William the Elder, supposedly until boy Harry came of age."

She put down her teacup. She flipped back her hair.

"But Mrs Start knew that the family's hold on the farm was precarious; to make their position stronger she married the 'caretaker' tenant, even though she disliked him. For three years he gave Harry and his sisters a hard time. Then, despite everything, William the Elder evicted them all just before Harry could come into his tenancy. Some pretext about the property being so run down it no longer fitted the old tenancy agreement. He installed a man named Ball. There's still Balls out at Start's Meadow today, I believe."

"How'd you know all that?" I asked.

"It's in the Community Archive for anyone to see. Cletchley Village Hall, the little room round the back. Jack Tamblyn keeps the key."

"Anyway," said Janie Powell. "Why would he shoot the Flower King if it was William the Elder who turned them out?"

"It may be – " said Howard Powell slowly – "it may well be that in wounding the son, he hoped to wound the father."

"Then," said Margaret Bath, "he didn't know the father."

"That's just it," I said. "He didn't, at all. Harry Start couldn't've ever've seen either William in the flesh."

"The Start eviction would have been conducted through Bowhays's land agent, it's true," said Howard Powell. "For that matter, an outlying tenant like Start would have had no reason to suppose there were two William Bowhayses."

"It was early morning in the fields when Harry Start came on the flower pickers," I said dramatically. "He was on the Bowhays estate. He had a pistol in his pocket and murder in his heart."

I looked around the table. I held them all in my hand – excepting only Mrs Teagarden, who was examining her nails.

"Harry Start saw a gentleman in charge. He asked the gentleman's name. A flower picker, a little girl, told him it was Mr William Bowhays Johns. Now he was sure of his man. The cause of all his family's troubles, in his sights at last. He waited. He followed on to Morden Quay. And there he—"

"Wrong William," said Janie Powell. "How – poignant. I do mean poignant, don't I? How—"

"How did you know that?" asked Margaret Bath. "I've never heard that story before."

"Because," I said, "I know the flower picker Harry Start spoke to that morning."

They all stared blankly. They were beginning to remind me of the fish heads on my plate. Suddenly I felt a bit bored with the whole thing. Too much explaining, not enough action. Then I remembered something. I got up and went in the house. I went in the hall, to the bowl of flowers on the spindly table at the foot of the stairs. There – I thought so – a few papery shapes, snapped off short to flatter the larger blooms. You'd hardly notice, really. I tweaked a couple out and dripped back round to the door. Everyone straightened quickly when I came outside again.

I struck a pose with the flowers for a second, like I was the Flower King in the picture. Then I flopped them on the table, the poor things.

"See these? They're a variety called Little Addie. Young Mr William named them for Addie Hand. Addie Hand was the girl Harry Start spoke to that morning, and *she* told me the story."

"Mrs Pinder," said Margaret Bath. "It's Mrs Pinder, isn't it?"

"It was good, the fishes and stuff," I said, backing off. "But I got to get back now."

It was almost twelve-fifteen. The Coalyards would be on their way up to the filling station – and today's would be a grudge match. The Portables had rubbished them the day before.

There was just one thing worth staying for. And that was –

"You know you said you had his journal, young Mr William's journal –"

"It's fascinating," said Howard Powell, his eyes locked in mine. "Fascinating. And it may just shed some light on this – it may just. Wait. I'll be right back."

He marched in the house. No one said a word. Then Margaret Bath said softly, "Poor Mrs Pinder."

Margaret Bath could see what had happened. She didn't need her *t*s crossed or her *i*s dotted. The Flower King had thought a lot of Mrs Pinder as a child. And poor Mrs Pinder had had a hand in what had happened to him, although she hadn't meant to. What Margaret Bath *didn't* know was, Pinny's vision in daffodil yellow, the vision of the Flower King falling at the very same time as he really was falling, down on Morden Quay – or perhaps *before* he fell. Margaret Bath wouldn't find *that* in the Community Archive. *That* was Planet Strange.

Suddenly the pinhead Afghan streamed out through the french windows. It made straight for Mrs Teagarden and flobbed its head in her lap and slubbered over her dress.

"Spree!" squawked Mrs Teagarden. "Get *down*! Spree!"

A dog. Called Spree. Definitely time to go.

Margaret Bath thought so, too. "Back to work," she said. She nodded over at the easel under the oaks. Would I like to see how it was going? I shook my head. I told her thanks, but I had to get back. I *did* have to get back.

Then she said, in a funny way, "Come a little way, at least." So I did.

We walked on a bit, out of earshot – then she turned. She nodded back at the loggia.

"It's thirty feet by eight. Guess how many lambs' knuckles in the floor."

I thought of a number. "Um … two – no, three thousand, four hundred and … seventy-two."

She laughed. "Way out." Then she got serious. "Come and see me, will you? Can you come Tuesday at four? It's about Mrs Pinder."

"Yeh…" Why not? Maybe she could help me get Pinny to Mount Hope. "Yeh, all right."

"I'm at Endacott – over Morden Pool, on the Quay road?"

"Oh, right. I know it."

Endacott. It figured. I'd seen her, odd mornings, painting in the morning mist by Morden Pool.

"I'll get on, then." I watched her swinging away across the lawns. Her hair swung like cloth from one side to the other as she walked. When her weight was on her right foot, it swung right. When she led with her left, it swung left.

She turned. "Eleven thousand, five hundred and twenty."

"What?"

"Bones in the floor."

"You're kidding," I shouted.

"Forty-eight to the square foot," she shouted back. "Four knuckles per sheep. That's a lot of lambs to floor the loggia. Think about it."

I walked back, thinking about it. It was a whole lot of sheep. It seemed to me they must have collected the bones from somewhere else, besides. Perhaps they asked the neighbours. Perhaps they had a whip-round. When I got back and sat down Janie Powell had melted away. It was me and Mrs Teagarden.

We waited, or at least I did, for Howard Powell and the Flower King's journal. At last Mrs Teagarden chocked the dishes together. She tipped the fish heads down for the dog, but it was too stupid to eat them. It flopped under the table like a dead thing. All the teacups jumped.

"Why's it called Spree?" I asked, not really interested.

"He was one of Mr Powell's little spending sprees," she said shortly.

She didn't say anything else, and neither did I. When she wanted to go in with a stack of dishes she found the french windows had swung to. She humphed a bit and looked round at me, but I was busy fixing my watchstrap at the time.

At last she blimped her way in with her backside and made a big deal of getting the dishes through. After she'd gone, it was me and the dog. I'm not much for dogs, so I wandered in. If I couldn't see Howard Powell, I'd nick off home.

As it happened, I did see him, almost straight away. It was a small room off the hall. There was a big desk slathered in papers, and a noise in the corner. I went in. The noise in the corner was Howard Powell being violent with a filing cabinet. He saw me come in and carried on as if he hadn't. Beside and behind him were piles of files.

I sat on the desk and looked around. Another dim room. Long casement windows, but hardly any light. I got up and looked out. A gloomy conifer had grown to block the sun. I went back and sat on the desk again. Howard Powell fought with the filing cabinet. It wouldn't let him open the second drawer down until he'd shut up the top one, in case it fell on him. He smashed the first drawer home and tore out the second.

I was sitting on a house plan. It showed a small place, three views – front, back and side – only they weren't called views, they were called "elevations". Front elevation, Mount Ho— Excuse me? Front elevation – Mount

Hope Cottage?

I moved a couple of books. In the bottom right-hand corner, in a fancy box, the drawing said: "Abel Moorman Associates. Extension to Mount Hope, Toy's Lane, Cletchley. Prepared for: Mr H.G. Powell."

I looked up in the same moment Howard Powell looked up. My head was as full as his eyes were empty.

"It's not here," he said simply, whacking a last file out on the floor. "I tucked the Bowhays journal in the Mount Hope file, and the Mount Hope file was *here* – " he thumped the second drawer down with the edge of his fist. The metal bonged in and cracked out. "And it's not here now. And I'd like to know *who moved it*." A little tweak of a movement in the doorway caught his eye and mine. Mrs Teagarden straightened. She flicked a speck off her dress. She smiled brightly.

"Are you running Janie to riding at two, or am I?" she asked. "Only, I *do* like to know what's going on."

I'll bet you do, I thought. I'll just bet you do. I wouldn't mind knowing, myself.

CHAPTER
EIGHT

Uncle Champion grinned wickedly. He fished out his Pontefract cakes and waved them under my nose. His tiny room at Needham's woofed of the anti-foot-rot stuff he sprinkled in all his shoes. Liquorice was just about the last thing I felt like, but I took some anyway. Uncle Champion was unusually sociable this afternoon.

"Where's your mother?"

"Gone for a perm."

"She only just had 'airdo, back along."

"Well, she's having another."

"Bleddy old clown hairdo, that's what I call it."

"Well it isn't, and you shouldn't."

Any old excuse. M had dropped me off to visit alone, the skiver. I reckoned on fifteen minutes of grief with Uncle C., then a good hour downstairs with Pinny. I had a lot to tell her.

The young care assistant flicked in the room like a bright handkerchief. She clapped a tray on Uncle Champion's bedside table. Three cups of tea, two digestives in each saucer.

"All right then, Jack?"

"All right now, me 'andsome." He patted his knee. "Let's have me cuppa, then. I never saw you this morning."

She brought him his tea. He had her wrist in his paw in a moment.

"You're slopping tea on your biscuits now, Jack."

"Biscuits be beggared. I got something for you, maid."

"Behave yourself, Mr Champion. The tea trolley's waiting."

He tightened his hold. He pumped her wrist up and down, trying to bring her closer.

"I got somethin' special," he hissed. "Something special, just for you."

"Please don't, Mr Champion, I've told you before—"

"In the wardrobe, there," said Uncle, nudging me with his foot. "Shift yourself."

I opened the wardrobe. Plenty of shoes and a couple of old jackets, Uncle's prickly-tweed specials, guaranteed to irritate.

"Bottom left, boy, bottom left," brayed Uncle Jack, bursting with impatience. "Fetch 'un over. There. These is for you, dear."

It was a hefty chocolate assortment in a florid box flashed with yellow ribbon.

"Mr Champion, you know I couldn't possibly—"

"What's couldn't about it? What's couldn't about a nice bit o' chocolate?"

"It's very nice, really, but I—"

"I know you women." Uncle Champion wagged a finger at her and smiled his oily smile. "All you women got a sweet tooth. You eat they soft centres and you'll be fat's a trout. Then you'll be moanin'."

He made her take them. She was pale with humiliation. Why couldn't he leave her alone?

"Well – " she said, because she had to. "Well – it's nice of you."

He covered her hand with his other paw. "No, dear," he said, as if she was doing him a big favour. "No, dear, it's nice o' *you*."

"Well – thank you."

At last he released her. Now she would feel obliged to put up with Uncle's little jokes, and plenty more presents where *that* one came from. I could just imagine the trouble she had with oily old Uncle Champion. He fancied himself a ladies' man at seventy-eight.

Uncle Champion still ran an old black Morris Minor, and he never let anyone forget it. He alone amongst the Needham's residents could get out and about as he pleased. Uncle

Champion's Morris was known and feared around Redmoor. Twice a week he tooled around the town, jawing with the good ole boys outside the newsagent, stocking up on tacky gifts to embarrass any woman under forty who came within striking range. He parked wherever the fancy took him, relying on his "Disabled" sticker for a sympathy vote with the traffic warden. He'd park in front of The Jamboree (double yellow lines), half on, half off the pavement – or smack on the corner by Bray's Wet Fish, where the Moorstock traffic swung around a blind bend.

"Here," I said, grabbing the third tea. "We won't be needing three, thanks. Mum's not coming till later."

She took the cup and smiled. It was a tired smile. I knew her a little. Her name was Elaine.

Uncle Champion was rattling in his wardrobe. He looked up and caught her before she got round the door.

"How's Mrs P.?" he asked.

"Oh. Ward Sister says she had a better night. Dr Carol thinks Wednesday or Thursday."

Uncle Champion grunted. "Good job."

She got out and closed the door.

"'Laine," bawled Unc. "'Laine."

She opened it again. "Yes, Mr Champion?"

"You on tonight? Bring me my cocoa?"

"No, Jack," she said. "It's Joyce on tonight."

"Oh 'ang."

"So don't try any of your tricks."

He grinned. "I'm savin' meself for you, me lover." He loved this kind of stuff. It was the whole point, really.

"Yes," she said. "Well."

She closed the door again and trolleyed off, her ordeal by smarm over for the day.

Uncle Champion winked broadly. "Over here, boy. See what I got."

I looked in the bottom of his grungy wardrobe. In back, behind his going-out shoes and his staying-in shoes and his driving shoes and his Sunday shoes, was a seedy stack of chocolates, gift-pack bath salts, tins of fancy biscuits, boxes of handkerchiefs, Turkish delight, fruit jellies and everything else naff no one would ever want to buy for themselves.

Uncle Champion reached in. He dragged out a thick box of peppermint creams, well past its sell-by date.

"See these? These are for Mrs P. when she comes out. And these –" he reached in again; clotted cream fudge, this time – "these're for Mrs P.'s birthday, Saturday week."

Suddenly I woke up. The anti-foot-root powder had been doing my head in.

"Mrs P.? Mrs Pinder's in hospital? She's not downstairs?"

He shook his head. "Took bad, Wednesday. Ambulance come eight o'clock Wednesday evening."

"Why? What happened?"

Uncle Champion closed his wardrobe heavily with his good arm. He made it back to the bed and troughed down his tea. I waited, alarm bells sounding all over. Was Pinny OK? *Would* she come back? Would I ever—

"Some fun we had, Wednesday morning," he said. "Some games, in the day room. Mrs P. was going 'ammer and tongs at Miss Cuthburt, and Miss Cuthburt's bangin' her arms round – like she does – and givin' it stick, and—"

"Was it the talc again?" I asked quickly.

He nodded. He cackled a bit. "Rare old ding-dong it was."

"Then what happened?"

"Didn't see no Catherine Cuthburt for dinner, because she shuts herself up tight in her room till tea, and she only come down then because Mrs P.'s taken bad in *her* room. Doctor Carol come at seven-thirty, ambulance come at eight. Then they had some caper with Miss Cuthburt on the stairs. 'Er was shouting blue murder on the stairs till gone nine."

"Where is she? Moorstock General?"

He nodded again. "Now girlie here says they'll let her go Wednesday or Thursday. Watch out for fireworks then, boy."

It seemed to me there'd be little danger of fireworks from poor Pinny when she came out of hospital. *Everything* was upside down, now.

"What's up with her? D'you know?"

"'Ad a flare-up, prob'ly." He shrugged. "Funny thing was, they found Mrs P.'s talc in her drawer when they were packing up for hospital. Exac'ly the same as Miss Cuthburt's. Same box, same everything. Exac'ly the same."

Why did it have to flare up *now*, the what-ever-it-was that was wrong with Pinny? Then again, she *was* eighty-four. Anything could happen.

What was happening now, I could see, was that I was going to be stuck with Uncle Champion for another whole hour. I'd nip round Slimeford's instead. Sam had Nintendo. I could meet M outside Snipz 'n' Curlz. But Uncle Jack was all fired up. How to get away? I'd say something to tee him off. He was pretty touchy, usually. It shouldn't be too difficult. In fact it was surprisingly easy.

I got up. "You shouldn't make Elaine take presents from you. She doesn't like it."

"Dun't do any harm. Women like a bit of a fuss."

"No," I said, "they don't. They know you're only doing it to get one over on them. Elaine hates it. Can't you see? It embarrasses her."

"All right," he glared. "Don't say no more."

He crumpled a bit over his bedside table. I was free to go. Suddenly I felt very mean. That's what Uncle Champion did best. He made you feel mean. But he wasn't all smarm.

Hadn't he got a present for Pinny, for when she came out of hospital? And one for her birthday – which was one more than I had?

As if to make me feel worse than I already did, he handed me something. An envelope, from his bedside drawer.

"Mrs P. gave me this for you." He pulled out his hearing aid and turned his back. "Tell Peggy I'll see her alone next week."

His back looked old and lonely. I didn't know what to say. Whatever I'd said, he wouldn't have heard it anyway. I knew then, if I hadn't known it before, that some things are better left unsaid.

I was halfway to Slimeford's before I looked in the envelope.

It was a greetings card with vague lilac flowers on the front. It must have been left over from Pinny's last flare-up, because the front said: HOPE YOU'RE FEELING BETTER – or at least, that's what it *had* said. Now everything but the "Hope" had been roughly scribbled out.

The original sender's name had been scribbled out, too. Inside, all it said, in wibbly Biro capitals, was: YOU PROMISED.

CHAPTER NINE

The next day was Easter Sunday, which isn't any different from any other day in our house. M put the kettle on at three. At ten past, Danny Harris and D blew in from the stores and settled over the papers.

Danny Harris works weekends in the stockroom. He fills the freezers, amongst other things. He does the Calor Gas compound most weekends, too, rolling the long red propane torpedoes in rows and sorting the smaller blue butane empties for collection.

And me? I do as little as possible. I was sorry I was in the kitchen with D and M already. In a minute, D would remember something I had to do – or if he couldn't, he'd find something. The thing about Sundays is, keeping a low profile. Melt in the background. Say nothing. That way you don't get dumped on.

I hid behind the Sport *Extra*, not really reading it at all. I was thinking about Pinny's birthday, Saturday week. I'd had an idea heading up like a boil all morning. It was obvious. The visit to Mount Hope would be on Pinny's birthday. That would give me plenty of time to think of something. I had a feeling I'd need plenty of time. Mount Hope, Saturday week. Somehow, I'd—

"Sports section," said D, flapping his hand my way without looking up.

I folded the paper quick and gave it into his open hand. He spread it and read it, still without looking up.

Danny Harris yawned. Then he mashed a jam tart in his mouth. Danny Harris was big and slow, but he worked like a train when he had to, which was whenever D was around. He did Dawe's weekends, and he did the fudge factory after school, as well. Danny Harris was so big, you could only look at one bit of him at a time. He was only a fifth-year, too. D liked it that way, because he didn't have to pay him too much. He'd've filled the whole place with fifth-years if he could.

"I wonder Sligo's never rung," said D suddenly.

"They did," said M. "Sligo's rung Friday."

D went mad red in a flash. Race and Sligo were D's solicitors. I made myself small, in the corner. I knew the signs only too well.

"Don't tell me nothing, will you?" asked D venomously. "No one tells me nothin' around here."

"It's going through," said M. "Eileen Roper said end of this month, beginning of next."

"Never mind Roper, where's Jim Sligo to? Where's exchange of contract to?"

"End of the month," repeated M. "It's goin' through."

"It better."

What this was about, was Pollock's. D had had his eye on the Pollock's Portable Buildings site next door for years. Then, eighteen months ago, Pollock's changed hands behind D's back. I thought he was going to bite a chunk out of the kitchen door, the night he found out. Then he discovered the new owners were upcountry folk trying their hand at a business like Pollock's for the first time.

D gave it six months, top. Eight months later, D heard a whisper. He rang Merv. Cousin Mervyn's an estate agent. Merv looked into it. By November last year D was laughing. His offer accepted, he crowed over extension plans for the stores – as well as the Portable Buildings, there would be garden supplies including patio furniture, barbeque sets, tubs, peat, pond linings, the works.

That was a few months back. Little, or nothing, had happened since Christmas. Now Jim Sligo was never in. Miss Roper took his calls.

Jim Sligo's letters were few and far between.

"P'raps," said D, "p'raps you'd kindly tell me straight off if anyone rings next time. *If* you got a moment."

"Oh, I got a moment. Can't you see me sunnin' meself on the patio with me feet up? I always got a moment."

I got up to go before it got any worse. But I had to cross the kitchen.

"Where d'you think you're going?" asked D.

"Out."

"Out where?"

"Just out."

"Well, you can stop out the back and trim a box o' cauliflowers."

I tried to burn him back with the same angry red he was throwing out at me. I tried to take it in, and torch it right out again – right there, at the top of his head.

"*What* did you say?" said D. "Come here and say that."

"*Nothing*," I said. "I'm going out back."

D flinched. "What's hot here? Ceiling's hot – is it? Peg – feel my head. Feel it? How's my head hot?

"How do I know how your head's hot?"

I trimmed three cauliflowers, then I threw down the knife. I jacked the bike over the fence with my heart in my mouth in case D heard. I waited. Then I climbed the fence. I waited again. Then I jumped on. I took Top Road with my head down, heading west. I settled into a steady rhythm and felt freedom in my face.

I saw the yacht, gleaming white on the water, from the top of the long hill to the Saint's Quay. I'd cycled a good three miles. I didn't know where I was going, but the Saint's Quay seemed as good a place as any.

The four o'clock tide was running as I ripped down the hill past The Ferryman Inn. Soon it would lick the wonderful yacht that waited like a dry biscuit by the quay.

"Look at her. Sick, isn't it?"

I hauled up the bike by the wall, not too near Janie Powell. But right away she shunted along towards me, with her ice-cream spotting the wall as she came. Away to the left, where the Saint's Chapel broke the wind, Mrs Teagarden fought a paperback on a plaid rug spread with picnic bits. She had on a strange white hat with a wide brim and no top, so her head showed through in the middle. With one hand, she held her hat. With the other, she clamped down her pages.

"I don't know," I answered. "Is it?" Janie Powell had had a fine contempt in her voice. I wondered how long she'd been stewing on the wall. I'd been stewing a bit myself, all the way over and down.

"She's *so* med-i-ocre. Guess what she's reading? Jilly Cooper. It's sick. She never thinks about *anyone* but herself."

"Tell me about it," I said bitterly. She looked a question over her ice-cream.

"My folks," I explained. "*They're* always looking after number one. My mum, she's got a mouth like a cash till. Slams open, slams shut, eats money. An' my dad's got a brain like one."

The beautiful yacht stirred against the quay. Her lovely white hull lifted blindly on the tide. Her name, on the aft end, rose with her. *Avatar* said the sporty red lettering shadowed in grey.

"Ava – who?" I asked, nodding towards her.

"*Avatar*." Janie Powell sighed. "Dad went to India last year. To an ashram."

"Ash – what?"

"An ashram. Oh … it's the SBGs. You know. Don't you know about the Sri Bindhi Group? An ashram's a religious community, and the SBG's one is near Delhi. My father went. And the Avatar Sri Bindhi touched him."

"Ava – who?" I said again. All I wanted to know was, why the boat had such a weird name. The way she looked at me, you'd think I was winding her up.

"An avatar," she said coldly, "is an incarnation of a Hindu god. And the Avatar touched Dad, and then he was – different. And when he got back, he bought the boat, because of the name."

"Why, didn't *he* call it that?"

She shook her head. "He said it was meant

106

to be, when he saw it. And when he got back from buying the boat, she got him to buy the house."

"She?"

Janie Powell nodded towards the figure on the rug. "*Her*. Mrs Teagarden. *She* wanted Stopeley. *She* wanted him down here, miles away from anywhere. Miles away from *me*. Before, it was always me and Dad. Now it's her and him."

"I thought she was just the housekeeper."

"So," said Janie Powell, "did I."

Eyeing Mrs Teagarden, she cracked into her cornet with a vengeance. There's some people you don't want to get the wrong side of. It seemed to me Janie Powell was one of them.

"I thought you got on," I said. "You and Mrs Teagarden. You were talking enough ridin' and stuff, the other day."

"Oh, yes," she said bitterly, "we get on. Dad likes everyone to get on. Mrs Teagarden wanted Dad to get on with her mother. Said she wanted to come down here to be near her. She's even got him to do up a cottage for her mother, so everyone gets on. It made me want to *throw* when he told me."

"Mount Hope?" I asked. "Mount Hope Cottage?"

She nodded. "She gets *everything* she wants." Then she turned. "How did *you* know?"

"I saw the plans for Mount Hope when – when the file with the journal went, you know, missing."

"Oh, yes," flashed Janie Powell. "The Mount Hope file. *Such* a shame. All the documentation for poor Mrs Teagarden's mother's cottage, all missing. Survey, deeds and everything. Pity I missed the –"

Suddenly she thought she'd said too much. She had. Way too much. I leaned in close. "What about the journal?"

"What about it?"

"Have you got it?"

"I haven't got anything. I just meant, it's a pity."

Brilliant orange-red. Her mouth and chin and neck and all the air around them, brilliant giveaway orange. Janie Powell was lying her face off – and for all the wrong reasons.

She shook back her hair and jumped up as Howard Powell waved from the yacht. He hopped on the quay, his big face red and shiny under a divvy captain's hat. I waved and smiled. Then I spoke quick and low, before the moment could slip away:

"What'd be nice, would be if the Bowhays journal came back. It hasn't got anything to do with Mrs Teagarden or anything. It was only tucked in the file. It'd be nice if it came back soon. I bet your dad doesn't go much on tipping the house up for nothing, does he?"

She flashed me a hard look as Howard Powell hove up. I was pretty sure she got the point.

"Who's for a turn on the tide?" huffed Howard Powell, all shiny and nautical, with his eyes watering in the wind. "Look lively, darling. Graham – can you crew?" He turned and waved. "Gaye! Come on! Gaye!"

But Mrs Teagarden waved her novel. "You go," she shouted. "Don't forget The Ferryman at eight."

"Missing you already," sang Howard Powell. Janie rolled her eyes. She mimed throwing up behind his back. Then she grinned. She was all right, was Janie. Bit devious. But all right underneath.

It was a wonderful evening. Once the stumpy little Saint's Chapel had hidden Mrs Teagarden from sight, we took off in more ways than one. We spanked along for a bit under a lot more sail than we needed, with the wind tearing our faces. She was showing off, but she didn't misbehave – the *Avatar* was sweet as a nut, even I could tell. She'd love you in a swell, or she'd tickle the dim flat river like a keen and lethal knife – it was all the same to her.

We took the tide all the way up to the Eggham Turn, which is almost, but not quite, to Morden; and the woods and the lime kilns bowled by. We raced by herons on silky mudflats, and we triggered them up in the sky as we went. We ran under grim old arsenic flues with our sails tight as eggs, thrumming a low and thrilling note. And a brisk southerly clapped in our clothes and hair and smacked the *Avatar* on as we shimmied the rig to catch it.

At last we motored back against the wind. My head felt three sizes bigger. My eyes felt like they'd drop out on deck. All the air'd been sucked out of my ears and pumped back in again behind my eyes.

Janie Powell sat bleakly at the bow. I noticed a moulded seat in the cabin roof. I tried it for a bit, blissing on what was probably eighty grand's worth of yacht under my backside. I was hoping to see someone – anyone – I knew, so I could wave, dead cool, from the stream-lined peak of a passing dream.

"Here a minute," said Howard Powell. "Take the helm."

Take the helm. I jumped over. I took it. Howard Powell sat heavily beside me.

"A good high freeboard and plenty of bum room," he said. "That's what you want."

Howard Powell was acting again. This time it was The Seasoned Sailor. Above us cracked a black flag. It showed a castle with a hawk over, and crossed swords under, in white on a black field. *The Defenders* logo, probably. Wasn't I helmsman for famous John Gently?

"The flower boats sailed to and fro here

once," said Howard Powell. "Or rather, fro. They would've brought other cargo upriver, and fruit and flowers down."

"Lime?"

"Too dirty for the flower boats. Passengers, probably. To port a bit, Graham." He sighed. "That journal never showed up. Nor the Mount Hope deeds. Ghastly stupid mess, really."

I wondered if Janie could hear. Her back looked taut and guilty.

"It'll turn up," I said loudly. "Can't be far away."

We went on a little way, then Howard Powell took the helm again and I sat in his place. The seat was warm. The river rushed by. I was as easy with Howard Powell as I was with Pinny – and he was easy with me. He made a big, easy space all around him, and in it I could be myself. I could've talked about anything under the sun, but I didn't. The one thing I found myself talking about was Pinny.

"You know Mrs Pinder I told you about, the flower picker? She's in hospital. But she's coming out Wednesday. Or Thursday."

"Well, I'm sorry, and I'm glad," said Howard Powell. "You think a lot of her, don't you?"

"Yeh," I said, "I do. It's her birthday, Saturday week. She's eighty-five. And what I'm doing is, I'm taking her up Mount Hope if it's all right, just to look. Because she used to live there."

"Did she now?" he said. "Fine by me. It used to be part of the estate, you know. Partly why I bought it."

"*If* I c'n get out of the house, that is," I added. I was in a funny mood. Maybe it was the *Avatar* under my feet. "And *if* I don't have to work."

"You work most Saturdays?"

"*Every* Saturday. I visit Uncle Champion afternoons – or sometimes in the morning. Work, or Uncle Champion. That's it, Saturdays."

He looked at me a couple of times thoughtfully. After a while he said, "We'd better be getting you home. Your parents'll be worrying about you."

"Fat chance," I said, as the stumpy Chapel showed us the Saint's Quay ahead, away to starboard over the reeds.

"I'd like to meet your Mrs Pinder," he said as he throttled back. "I'd like to hear her story sometime. Janie! Ready astern!"

At last we climbed into the car. It had taken a good forty minutes to put the *Avatar* to bed. We left her nodding by the Quay with the darkness closing around her.

Howard Powell dropped me off on the Top Road at nine-fifty, which was late enough already. I'd stowed the bike on the *Avatar*, too naffed to tackle the hill.

The street lights glared Howard Powell yellow as I came around the car. But still the green showed through. Hadn't the Hindu god, the Avatar Sri Thingy, touched him, somewhere in India? Maybe *that* was why he was green.

"I'll drop your bike up," he said. "Nice little run upriver, wasn't it?"

"Yeh," I said. "The best."

"We'll do it again sometime."

Please, I flashed, in my head. *Yes, please.* "It was excellent," I said.

He turned in the station forecourt and powered smoothly back the way we'd come, back to join Janie and Mrs Teagarden at The Ferryman, I supposed. I wished I were going with him. I wished I was going anywhere but home. I jumped the fence and sneaked around back, but I needn't have bothered. M was on it, straight away.

"Where've *you* been?"

"Just out."

"Just out," repeated M nastily. "You've not been out with them cauliflowers, have you?"

"I'll do them in the morning."

"I said, where've you been?"

"Nowhere. Out on the bike."

"You've been gone since three. I'm not stupid."

"All right. I've been sailing a thirty-five foot

113

performance yacht up the river and back."

"You nick off like that again, I'll sail you up the river. I haven't stopped long enough to whistle this afternoon. Danny did the caulis, an' I did Danny's freezer, thank *you* very much."

I miked a mini-pizza and some tired-looking chips I found by the fryer. When M cleared off for a bath I made up a whole packet of Angel Whisk and gobbed the lot. I finished up with two big spoonfuls of peanut butter and went upstairs, killing footfalls as I went, in case D heard me go.

I watched a film in bed until half-eleven. Then I switched off the light. After a while, tossing and turning, I thought I'd visit Pinny. Hadn't I scorched D's head with his own bad temper? Hadn't I thrown red out, as well as picked it up? How could I tell what else I might be able to do unless I tried? Maybe I could throw out something else. Maybe I could do Pinny some good.

I thought a bit. I pictured Moorstock General. I could picture it pretty well, because of visiting Uncle Champion there. Then I made myself green all over. When I was ready, I rose up out of myself, glowing green, and almost at once I was going in at the door – Ward 9 it was, the same ward Uncle Champion stopped in – and I was walking, walking and glowing, down along all the beds, and then I saw her.

The green rolled up and over her without me trying at all, up and over her bed and warmly over her poor sad head where it fuzzed the pillow with thin white hair. Without even trying, I pulsed a lovely green wave across her, top to bottom. I rippled green around her head and set a glow to match around the lump beneath, warmly, like a blanket.

I held it as long as I could. Then, gently, I pulled something back. I glowed off, passing the beds in reverse order. I passed through the Ward 9 doors like a ghost. I glowed down the corridor, the stairs, the corridor again. The main desk, casualty, reception – and out. I knew it was important to do the whole thing, but I didn't know why.

Then I was back in myself again, in my own bed, warm and full. I didn't know what it was that I'd done – but I knew I'd done Something.

CHAPTER TEN

"Cletchley 30056."

"Hello. Is that – is that Margaret Bath?"

"Speaking."

"It's me. It's about tonight."

"Sorry?"

I lowered my voice. "I'm ringing from Dawe's. It's about me coming to Endacott tonight. It's just, I can't make it, not tonight."

"Oh, don't worry. How about Thursday?"

"I can't get out at all this week. I got jobs. I think I could make it Monday."

"Monday next, then – at six?"

"OK." I was thinking furiously. I was grounded the rest of the week, but I could weasel out Monday next, if I had to. And I *did* have to. There were things I needed to ask Margaret Bath. Quite a few things, in fact.

"Howard tells me you had a trip on the river

on Sunday."

"Oh. Yeh. It was great."

"You took the helm, I hear. She's a lovely yacht."

"She is, yeh. The thing is, I've been thinking about Pinny's birthday—"

"I saw Mrs Pinder today. She's back to Needham's on Friday. She sends you her best."

"Is she? I mean, does she? I just put a card in the post."

"I took her in a big Easter egg. She laughed. She always liked a bit of a laugh."

"Have you known her a long time, then?"

"I used to look after her. Didn't I tell you? I used to work night shift at Needham's. We artists must scrape along somehow, you know."

"Anyway. She's better."

"Well, she's eighty-four, of course. But the nurse I spoke to said she picked up Monday morning. They were worried about her blood pressure on Sunday, but it came down overnight. They didn't think it would, but it did. Then Monday morning she sat up and had a full breakfast. They fetched Doctor Carol down to see."

Oh, I thought. Oh, wow. Sunday night. Sunday, glowing Sunday. My heart was beating like a hammer.

"You know the picture in the daffodil field?" I managed. "The daffodils picture. Did you finish it?"

"I'm working on it. You can see it Monday, when you come."

"Sorry I couldn't make it tonight."

"That's all right. Monday's better for me. There's someone I'd like you to meet."

"There is?"

"Monday, at six. Bye for now."

"See ya."

By Wednesday, I'd had enough. I'd split boxes in the stockroom. I'd been down Doney's Hardware getting creosote for D. I'd switched the posters in the video hire and chased shopping trolleys over the car park up to Pollock's and back. I'd sweated over one of the store windows with a stepladder, an old vest and a bottle of Mr Shiny. I'd done up bread orders for Monday. I reckoned I'd more than made up for nicking off Sunday afternoon.

After tea, I said, "I'm going up to watch telly. There's a film on."

I put the telly on in my room. About six forty-five I slipped out the back and went up Youth Club. I didn't say. I just went. It was easier that way.

All the way up through the estate I was thinking. Pinny and Mount Hope. Mount Hope and Pinny. How to get her there? Number one, Uncle Champion. Numbers one, two and three, Uncle Champion. I didn't even consider asking M. She wouldn't have done it, anyway. Worse still, she'd have stopped me doing it.

It had to be Uncle Jack. After my last visit I wasn't exactly best placed to ask him a favour. *And* he never drove further than Redmoor. But Mount Hope was only three, maybe three and a half miles. Uncle Champion was my best – my only – bet. I would have to play my cards right. I'd go in this Saturday and set it up for Saturday next. Then I'd prime Pinny. I pictured her face when I told her.

Suddenly Barf and the Portables – or two of them, anyway – swung round the corner ahead. I'd a lot rather they hadn't. Dawe's and everyone connected weren't exactly flavour of the month with the Portables since news of Pollock's sale to D had leaked out.

"Here it is," said Barf, coming right up. "Dawe, son of Dawe's World Domination. Why dun't he just buy up the village and have done?"

"What?" I said. "Who?"

"Your old man. He laid us off."

"He did? When?"

"He came in Pollock's yesterday and gave me 'n' Dean 'n' Snuff the push. A month's notice, from the end of this week. Right, Dean?"

Dean shrugged. "I'm goin' Dousland Carpets in July. Me brother fixed it."

"All right for some," said Snuff darkly.

"Can't he keep you on?" I asked. "Who's he going to get? Did he say? Did he—"

"I said, I know the business, Mr Dawe," said Barf. "I got two years in flexi-units and garden sheds. You won't get no one knows the business better."

"Yeh, and what'd *he* say?"

Barf reddened. "He said, I wouldn't keep *you* on, Bartlett, if you was Business Brain of the Year."

"There again," said Snuff, "you *did* reverse over his Fiesta."

For a moment Snuff kept a straight face. Then he and Dean cracked up. They meant the time Barf had remodelled the front of D's new Fiesta with the back end of a fully-loaded Pollock's lorry.

"That wasn't my fault," said Barf. "Me mirrors was angled wrong."

"I'm sorry, Barf," I said. I was, I was really sorry. "I hope you get something else."

"An' I hope your old man fouls up," spat Barf. "I hope he goes down the toilet."

"Yeh," I said, "so do I."

Barf gave me a funny look, but I was through them and past them and on the corner already. He shrugged. I watched them go. Barf looked back at me, once.

There weren't many at the Youth Club that night. We doubled in midfield and were still a winger short each side. Jamie Tree barked his knee on the path. Paul Doney scored five times. My sweater was wet when I picked it up to go in. It'd marked goal, along with Sean Pike's coat, at the muddy end of the field.

I bought Coke and crisps for me and Jamie Tree out of the three pounds twenty I'd lifted earlier from the stores' till. It's not like it sounds. I only charge 'em eighty pence an hour – pretty reasonable, really. I'd worked a good four hours that day, probably more. Lorraine was cool. She'd turn a blind eye to the till. She knew D wasn't about to pay me for anything. Gwen was cool, too. So long as I made the till roll balance, why should she care?

All I did was take for something big when M wasn't around. I'd serve someone with quite a few items, then ring in three pounds twenty pence – or whatever it was – less. The old till in the corner was best, you couldn't easily make out the display from the other side of the counter.

I played a rubbish game of snooker with Duncan Pengelly's sister. Then I played an even more rubbish game with Duncan Pengelly. If Duncan Pengelly had a brain he'd be danger-ous. The "Shoop Shoop" song – original ver-sion – was shooping as loud as Mr Tancock's tinny old jukebox would go. Then we had the Beatles – "Eight Days a Week". We have a lot of Sixties stuff at Youth Club. Mr Tancock's big on Sixties stuff. I don't mind it, myself. Some of it's pretty good.

We tipped out at nine. I hung around the field a bit with Jamie Tree. Then I started home. It must have been about twenty past nine when I came down the hill on the filling station. The stores were shut and dead. So was my bedroom window, opposite. I should've left the light on. I wondered if M and D had noticed I'd gone.

First I heard laughing. Then running footsteps – over in the car park. More footsteps – a shout. I jogged along the outside wall. I leapt it and crossed the forecourt like a leopard. I rounded the corner in time to catch Barf in front of the plate glass window with his arm raised like Steve Backley about to release a javelin, in the moment of throwing. Snuff and Dean hung watching in the shadows.

"Leave it!" barked Snuff, leaving it rapidly himself. Barf's rock hit the concrete. Dean melted away. Was he ever there? Barf pelted off after him like a windmill, head down. They were gone before the rock he'd dropped finished rolling on the concrete.

I picked it up. It was quite a big rock. I found Barf's spot. Not bad, but too far. I went closer. It was a good spot to throw from. Not too near to get hurt, not too far to miss a spectacular result. I brought back my arm like Steve Backley. Then I went for the ninety-metre mark.

The rock hit the window just left of centre with a bang that fired white cracks across the plate glass like instant frost. Somewhere in my head I heard a terrific peal of breaking glass and, through it, an alarm bell ringing. The rock bashed on through the shop, hitting something heavy inside. Seconds later a tooth of plate glass the size of Cornwall dropped like a dagger with a final, shattering sound I had a feeling I'd never forget.

My legs started moving on their own. They took me in the shadows, round the back of the stockroom. They took me down the hill and under the bridge and across the road. They brought me up on the other side and right, on Downlake Road, and left again off it, down the lane backing the terrace gardens. They brought me swiftly through the back gate, and swiftly in at the door. They carried me noise-lessly up the stairs, even as the living room door was opening. They brought me to the edge of my bed. Then they went completely.

The telly was still on. I watched a pro-gramme about classic cars for a bit. I had to turn the sound up. There was a lot of door-banging and shouting downstairs. The alarm bell from across the road was pretty annoying. I ate the Bar Seven I'd bought at Youth Club. I switched channels and settled for the sports quiz. Suddenly the alarm bell stopped. My ears rang on for a minute or two. But no alarm bell was worse. It meant that D was out there doing something, mad red and wild as a pit bull. I killed the sports quiz and the light in one lunge and dressed for bed.

After a while I heard shouts across the road and something heavy being dragged. I'd name Tarmouth strikers since '85 in my head. Then I'd open the curtains.

D and Mr Hocking from next door were manhandling a big sheet of hardboard over the window. The shop door was open. The forecourt lights were on. D looked shorter than he usually did. He had on his rancid-green nylon boiler suit. It was probably the time he'd taken getting into it that had saved me on the stairs.

I watched them haul the hardboard on the sill. I watched D nail it in place, seven nails one side, seven nails the other. It didn't cover the window top to bottom, but it stretched from side to side and masked the hole. It was only the side window by the door – big enough, but nowhere near as big as the one in front. It was the window I'd sweated over half the afternoon.

I watched D bring something out. He showed it to Mr Hocking. Mr Hocking took it. He weighed it in his hand. D pointed to a spot in front of the window. Mr Hocking turned. He handed D the rock. D looked around, as if he'd see where it came from.

I dropped the curtain and lay back in bed.

I tried to feel as though I'd just smashed my own family's store. I tried to feel it was my fault my dad was fighting hardboard and his own bile across the street, but it seemed to me it was his.

I heard the breaking glass inside my head. I saw the rock bashing, the white cracks starring, the big tooth falling. There were no two ways about it. It felt just great.

CHAPTER ELEVEN

"Must've been quite a bang," said Gwen conversationally. She set the rock back down on the counter. "I said, must've been quite—"

"It was. Shift your feet out, will you?" Flat on his back, D tweaked out the last nails gripping the smashed side of the counter. His boiler-suited legs stuck out from under, the knees dark with oil right through to the trousers beneath.

My rock had killed the counter and finished up in the motor oil. At least two plastic litre bottles had split over the floor. The red and white check vinyl was tacky underfoot, despite two buckets of hot soapy water and M's best effort. It was still only eight-thirty. M had retired with her buckets for a cuppa. I was glad I hadn't seen her, down on her hands and knees. I might've felt a twinge, and I couldn't afford twinges. It was them or me.

Gwen picked up the rock again. She loved a bit of drama. Her teeth glistened, her mouth clacked. She couldn't stop.

"Take you long to shift the glass, then? You got to be so careful with broken glass. Mother put her hand through a glass door once—"

Suddenly she dropped the rock on the counter, right over D's head. The boiler-suit legs jumped.

"Leave that rock go, will you?" barked D. "Get a bucket and take out the shelves by the door for bits of glass. And set that rock where I c'n see it. I got Bill Dent at two."

Suddenly I had a mega-twinge. Constable Dent, at two o'clock. I hadn't thought about what might happen after I'd thrown the rock – I'd just thrown it. I hadn't thought about floor-scrubbing or counter-dismantling or – worst of all – Constable Dent. I backed out slowly by the card stand before D realized I was there.

I was under the bridge and halfway down the hill before I knew where I was going. It had to be Doney's Hardware. Paul Doney's a mad-house, he is. But he's trusting and stupid and lends me stuff. *And* he doesn't ask questions.

The valley opened before me as the hill switched west. The river was gone, the woods were gone. All that showed was the top of Leigh Crags with its scrawny black conifers, like vultures round a bone. It was one of those magic mornings. The valley was up to its neck in soft white even mist, surprise mist like Christmas you didn't expect, sharpening my breath with its own and making a strange land where the bridge and the river and the village used to be.

I looked back. Way above me Stopeley Rise winked creamy-white in its trees. Somewhere beyond, where the mist couldn't hide it, Dawe's Filling Station was picking up the pieces. *This* morning, of all mornings, M wouldn't have noticed if I'd emigrated. I thought about it, once or twice, on the way down the hill. I'd sailed a yacht and smashed a window. What could happen next?

I stopped for a breather by the Boys Brigade Hut. Its peeling blue-paint doors were thick with washed-out posters, one on top of another. The Boys Brigade door was the village notice board. Whatever was happening – and there wasn't much – it would be on the Boys Brigade door.

The fluorescent orange poster topmost of all shouted the Youth Club Disco, second of May. Its bottom left-hand corner took out the time and date of the car boot sale on the notice underneath, but it'd probably come and gone. I lifted the corner to see. It had. Also gone were the Cletchley W.I. Pot Luck Supper on Feb. the twenty-seventh, Catatonic supported by Eat My Dog at Cletchley Village Hall, and "A Life in the Valley" – speaker: Margaret Bath. I took a closer look – wouldn't you?

"Discover *your* village as it once was. Member of Redmoor Local History Group Margaret Bath draws on her extensive knowledge of the Valley for this fascinating glimpse of Cletchley's past. Long memories especially welcome! All proceeds to Cletchley Archive."

When I'd read everything it had to say I buried it under the Youth Club poster again. It seemed to me Margaret Bath could do worse than strip down the Boys Brigade door for a glimpse of Cletchley's past. There were probably posters saying "Careless Talk Costs Lives" or "Dig for Victory" right on the bottom.

I was lucky. Paul Doney was still in bed. After we broke the toaster – I don't know how – we cycled up on the scramble trail on Cletchley Old Mine, me on Paul Doney's brother Philip's spammy old ten-speed, and spent the morning breaking a course on the spoil.

After that, I had to go home. Doney had the dentist *and* a haircut that afternoon. I'd almost rather've gone to the dentist myself than go home. But I had to be in for lunch. Not being in for lunch was a good way to draw D's attention more surely than anything else.

It was around half-one when I ducked round the door. Both M and D were at the kitchen table over empty plates and a pot of tea. There were no newspapers on the table.

They were just sitting. It was so unusual to see them sitting quietly together at lunch time – or at any time – that I didn't know what to say.

"I got a little show for you," said D ominously.

"I've been down the Hardware," I said airily. "Thought you might've wanted to know if they had that other wood preservative stuff you were on about the other—"

D jumped up. "Don't wood preservative me, boy. Watch this."

He snapped on the telly. He hit PLAY on the video recorder – a new video recorder – a Haiku Sonic, matt black, bit like Hocking's one next door. Ours must've packed up at last. I wanted to ask if he'd bought it new. But D threw me an ugly look to see if I was watching.

M scraped me out a chair. She poured me a cup of tea. She didn't look at me at all. The lid fell off the teapot onto my mug when she poured. She didn't pick it up.

The air over D's head rippled like a heat haze on a summer's day – only the heat-haze over D was red of the ugliest kind. There was something else in that room as well, but something was stopping me getting it.

"All right now, matey?" asked D unpleasantly. "Sitting comfortably, are we?"

The telly showed a black and white picture of – concrete. And someone's foot. With rising panic I saw it was mine. It was a bird's-eye view, as though the camera was on a building, looking down.

The figure onscreen bent down. It picked something up. The picture cut to another camera as the figure walked out of shot. This time the view was a bit above eye-level, full-on to the figure. The figure brought back its arm like Steve Backley. It braced itself for a throw. It looked up. It was unmistakably me.

D jumped up. "YOU GOT A SCREW LOOSE OR SOMETHING?" he blared at the top of his voice. "I SAID, YOU GOT A SCREW LOOSE OR SOMETHING?"

Behind him, the figure onscreen threw the rock with all its might. It stood a moment, stupidly. Then it turned and ran.

I had completely forgotten D's video surveillance. I'd never had a reason to remember it before. I'd forgotten it so completely I'd never even been worried this would happen. Now it was happening. What could I do?

"What kind of fool d'you think I'd look if Bill Dent saw THAT? Callin' in Bill Dent, and it's only ME OWN BOY'S been hooliganisin' the place. WHAT KIND OF FOOL D'YOU TAKE ME FOR?"

"Why didn't you look at the tape *before*, then?" I countered recklessly. "Last night, before you rang Bill Dent?"

"Because I only had to wait till this morning

an' borrow Hocking's video to PLAY it on, DIDN' I? Because when I come in twelve o'clock last night the tape wouldn't play on ours, WOULD IT?"

"I only cleaned off the tape-heads—"

"We'll clean off YOUR 'ead for yer, shall us?"

"*All right,*" said M, cutting across him like a knife. "All right, Derek. Sit down." We all sat down, D last of all. I was careful to sit so M was between him and me.

"Someone put you up to it?" asked M. "What did you think you were doing? Takin' a stone and throwing it through the store window. What did you *think'd* happen? Think it'd bounce off or something?"

"No," I said. "I didn't think about—"

"HE'S OFF HIS HEAD, HE IS," raved D, completely off his. "He wants putting up St Anne's, he does—"

"No one put me up to it," I cut in. "I just picked it up and did it. I didn't plan it. It just happened."

"You just picked it up and did it," repeated M. "Know how much a plate glass window like that costs?"

"No, I—"

"And a counter? *And* a shelving unit?"

"You c'n claim money off of them for it, can't you? What does *he* pay the insurance man for?"

He came up out of his chair at me like a volcano. I grabbed the teapot and held it in front of me. But I wasn't afraid. I had things I could do. Besides, the air had changed. I could see what it was in that room between the three of us that I hadn't seen before. It was lonely, lost, where-did-we-go-wrong? blue.

"You don't think nothin' of it, do you," asked D in a strangled voice, "what we built up? The station, and the stores. You don't think nothin' about it at all – do you?"

"I do," I said. "But it's not the only thing."

"You're too good for the stores, are you?" asked M. "You got better things to do, have you?"

I looked at them both, and I remembered Black William. William the Elder, with his bright and greedy eyes. "Get what you want," Black William had said. "Get what you want – and keep it." But I wouldn't be like him. I wouldn't be like them.

"Find what you love," I said. "Find what you love – and do it." I put the teapot softly on the table. I backed out, up to my room. They didn't say a thing. There was nothing left to say.

CHAPTER
TWELVE

Janie Powell looked jumpy as a hedgehog under a bonfire. She'd climbed out of the Defender Series Land Rover just a moment before. I thought I'd heard something expensive pull onto the forecourt. It was seriously flash and carelessly parked – and it had my bike on the roof rack.

Janie Powell looked all around. She walked up and down. She looked a bit desperate to me. I knocked on my bedroom window. Bit stupid, really. Of course she wouldn't hear me with the Saturday traffic chuffing by.

I pressed my face on the window and watched Howard Powell fight the roof rack. He walked round and tried to free up the bike on the other side. I could see he was swearing a bit. I'd have gone right over to help, except for my Holiday Project. And D.

My Holiday Project was Energy. Or something. I'd lost the worksheet, back along. I rang Jamie Tree. He read me the topic:

"List some different examples of renewable and non-renewable sources of energy. Is your house energy-efficient? How many items in your house consume energy? How many conserve it? Draw an energy curve for your house. How do you think it could be improved? Choose a method of energy generation and write about it in detail. Mention points in its favour and points against. How do you think energy will be generated in the year two thousand and twenty?"

Just reading the question consumed *my* energy. I'd made a start, spread out on the bedroom floor. But my mind kept hopping around. Saturday again – and not just any Saturday. It was the Saturday I would set up Uncle Champion for the visit to Mount Hope. Nothing must go wrong. It had almost gone wrong last night. M had almost derailed the whole thing, over a mug of Quik-Choc late last night.

"You got to stop over the house out of Dad's way," she started. "Just until he cools off, all right?"

I nodded miserably.

"Got some school work to do?"

I nodded miserably again.

"Best get on with it, then."

She thought a bit. "Don't get out much, do you?"

I shrugged. She just told me I had to stay in. What did she think? Then she said, "I got to go to Tarmouth tomorrow. I'll drop you in town. You can see a film. Like that?"

This was worse than anything. I'd expected everything *else* to get in the way of my seeing Uncle Champion – but I hadn't expected niceness.

"Take Paul or Jamie if you like. You can go up Whoppa King for dinner, an' I'll meet you five o'clock after a film. Like that, wouldn't you?"

"No," I said, "I wouldn't. I don't feel like it."

"Get out. You'll like a film. I'll get the paper, see what's on."

"I don't *want* to see a film. I want to visit Uncle Champion like we usually do."

"Shan't you like town, then?"

"No. I like Uncle Champion."

"Can't think why," M'd said, clattering up the mugs and blowing the niceness bit completely. "He dun't like you."

Janie Powell looked my way. I waved. She saw me. *She* waved. Then she beckoned. I thought a moment. I could make out D over in the stores, doing a Mr Shiny on the front window with his disgusting old vest. So I was banned from the shop. I could go in the car-

136

park though, couldn't I? I wouldn't go *in* the stores, I'd stay outside. Had to get my bike back, didn't I?

Suddenly I decided. I hurdled my Holiday Project and triple-jumped the stairs, peeling a page on wind farms: advantages of, off my shoe at the bottom. I stuffed it by the phone. Later.

By the time I'd dodged the traffic over the road Howard Powell had lifted down my bike and propped it by the pumps. He looked a bit like a petrol pump himself. The veins stood out on his head. His face was red and shiny.

"What *took* you so long?" asked Janie Powell.

"Ah!" said Howard Powell, "Graham! I'm glad we caught you. We were wondering – weren't we, Janie? – if you'd give us the pleasure of your company next Saturday. We're moving the *Ava* to semi-permanent moorings at Morden Quay. Bring a friend if you like. Cletchley Quay, two o'clock."

My mind turned over like a BMW ignition, making a couple of lightning connections at once. Cletchley Quay, at two. Visiting hours at Needham's – three till five. It couldn't be done.

"It's Mrs Pinder's birthday next Saturday," I mumbled. "I'm taking her up Mount Hope."

"Mrs Pinder! Love to meet her! We'll take her with us on the *Ava*, bring her down the river like a queen. We can look in at Mount

Hope afterwards, if you like. Then tea at Stopeley to finish. How's that?"

That was unexpected, amazing – everything a generous surprise *should* be. I loved the man.

"That'd be *amazing*, if we could. She'd *love* it, but – she's pretty old."

"We'll take it steady. Make a day of it. What d'you say?"

I pictured Pinny on the river, where the flower-boats had blazed with daffs for Tarmouth. *Would* she be OK? I pictured her on the *Avatar*, comfy in the cabin-roof seat, cruising the terraced market slopes like – like a queen, Howard Powell said.

"I say *yeah*!"

"Proper job," winked Howard Powell. "What do you say, Janie?"

"Is Mrs Teagarden coming?"

"I should think so, yes," he said mildly. "Why?"

"Oh, nothing. I may as well come, I suppose."

He watched her keenly a moment. To break the tension, I asked, "Why Cletchley Quay? I thought you were down the Saint's."

"We were. Had a wonderful run up to Leigh Rock on Wednesday. Moored at Cletchley Quay on the way back. Too much company at Cletchley, so I'm taking six months at Morden – that your father inside? I'd better just clear it with him."

"No…" I said desperately, "it'll be OK. He – he won't want to be bothered with it. Really. It'll be…"

But he was crossing to the stores already. He was opening the door. He was going in. I saw D's hand drop from the window inside as he turned to Howard Powell.

Janie Powell fussed in her bag. D eyed me once, through the window. It had been a magic carpet ride, those few minutes when Pinny and I had been going sailing on Saturday. Now the carpet was about to be whisked away.

"Here," hissed Janie Powell, bringing something square from her bag. "It'll look funny if I put it back now. I don't know how. You keep it."

She flipped open the scarf it was wrapped in. It was a leather-bound book, gold-edged, heavy, important.

"What is it?"

"What d'you think? *You* wanted it."

She fanned its pages. Leggy brown copperplate handwriting crowded every line. "William Arthur Bowhays Johns" said the flyleaf, in more of the same. I couldn't believe it. She was offering me the Flower King's journal.

But I had a firm grip on this one. I needed more trouble like a poke in the eye with a sharp stick. I knew exactly what to do.

"I'm not touchin' it. Take it home and put it back."

She sighed. "I didn't mean to take the stupid thing, anyway. I didn't know it was in with the other stuff."

"What about the Mount Hope stuff? Shouldn't you give it back?"

"I can't, now. Dad thinks he must've left it in London. I can't just put it back. He'll know it was me."

"Can't you stuff it behind a chair or something?"

"I thought you wanted this," she said coldly. "I thought you were going to tell Dad if it didn't turn up."

It was tempting, I'll admit. When I wouldn't take it, she laid it on the ground.

"I'll leave it here then, shall I? I don't want it. *You* don't want it."

I backed off. "I'm not touching it," I said firmly. "I want to see it, but you got to *put it back*."

She eyed me steadily. We both knew who stood to lose. At any moment Howard Powell might come bowling out of the stores. He was a long time coming. I thought I heard raised voices. Probably D chewing out Danny Harris.

I almost took up that journal. It turned me over to see it lying on the oily concrete like a lame bit of junk no one wanted. But I stopped myself in time. What was I? Stupid? Janie

Powell felt guilty. Now she wanted to put the guilt on me. I had more than enough of my own.

Suddenly she snapped. "Thanks for nothing." She swiped it up and jammed it in her bag.

I caught a wave of purple. I saw she was close to tears. "You could always—"

"Always what?"

Someone was shouting in the stores. Someone else was shouting back. There was Something Going On.

"What is it?" asked Janie Powell. "Where's Dad?"

"I don't know," I said. "Come on."

We burst in the door. Behind the half-a-counter stood Danny Harris and Gwen. I met Gwen's eye over the till. The eye was boggling. Her mouth was open so far, her chin was almost on the floor. She brought up her finger. Ssssh. I sidled in beside her.

"He in't goin' NOWHERE," D was shouting. "Not sailin', not NOWHERE. The boy's a lunatic."

"Graham's a very sensitive lad," said Howard Powell. "All work and no play, you know, makes Jack a dull—"

"Graham? Graham who?"

"Your son has a very lively imagination."

"Oh, yer. He *imagines*," said D sarcastically. "He *imagines* he c'n do whatever he likes an'

141

get away with it."

"I find him courteous and helpful," said Howard Powell stiffly, "if a little repressed."

"Who's repressed? What's he been sayin'? He been moanin'?"

"He doesn't have to. I can see."

"Oh. You can see, can you? Well, you won't have no trouble seein' the door then, will you? *Mister* famous big-shot whoever-you-are."

I couldn't believe he'd said it. I felt every word in my chest. Gwen caught her breath. She nudged me in the arm. I nudged Danny Harris. He nudged me back. The nudge travelled back to Gwen in the space of time it took Howard Powell to draw himself up.

"Horrible little man," burst Janie Powell. "Tell him he can—"

"My daughter seems to think you're a horrible little man," said Howard Powell loftily. "You have an extraordinary son. Let's hope he improves on his fa—"

Suddenly D squirted his bottle of Mr Shiny. The window-cleaner fluid took Howard Powell full in the face. It spittled his glasses. It spotted his collar and jacket. He looked as though he'd sneezed a monster sneeze.

"Dad!" squeaked Janie Powell.

"That'll clean off yer windows for you," said D nastily. "That'll clean 'em off nice."

Quick as a whippet, Gwen scooped a spray-can from the Motor Accessories bargain bin.

"John Gently!" she called. Howard Powell turned. She buzzed it across with amazing accuracy.

He caught it neatly in one hand. "Thank you," he said. "Miss Zest."

He levelled the nozzle at D's chest. But D had lost his nerve with Gwen's amazing throw. He sensed it. The mood was against him. He wondered why. He looked around. Three or four regulars were enjoying the scene from the third aisle across.

Dolly Gillet had forgotten whatever it was she'd wanted in the end freezer. Mr Tancock was feeling apples and putting them back in the onions. Mrs Pengelly was filling her trolley in slow motion with stuff that Ben, three, was handing her. Someone coughed. Ben dropped a tin.

"Just jokin'," shrugged D. "No offence." He checked the watching faces. No one was laughing.

"People like you," said Howard Powell grimly, "*are* an offence. I *could* present you with my dry-cleaning bill. Or I could simply…"

Suddenly he let fly with the spray-can. It was Hamnet's Bodywork Retouch, in Rustproof Flamenco Red: matches most popular cars. He emptied it thoroughly over D's overalls. It took a minute or two to get an even coat. When he'd done, he jammed the can in D's upper left pocket and patted it down.

"Guaranteed to cover most bodywork defects," he said. "But you'll have to live with the face. Come on, Janie. Let's go."

Gathering Janie, he swept past Motor Accessories. He reached the door. Gwen was waiting. She held up her hand, palm out. He clapped it with his.

"Defenders," he said.

"To the End," said Gwen.

I caught his wink, for me and me alone, before the door batted back. Howard Powell was gone – and we all seemed smaller for it.

D looked a bit like a pizza. He glistened. The calculator in his top pocket, the Biros in the other, the popper-studs on his overalls, his shirt collar under, his window-rag, his Mr Shiny and his watch – everything glistened tomato-red. A bit of cheese on the top, an olive in each ear, he'd be Dinner to Go.

Danny Harris sniggered.

"Give 'un another coat!" cackled cracked old Dolly Gillet. "Missed a bit, din' he? Give 'un another!"

It was Danny Harris who started the slow handclap. Then Gwen joined in – and so did Mr Tancock. One by one they all did, even Lorraine in the video hire. Dolly Gillet whumped the top of the freezer in time. They clapped D the length of the aisle, they clapped him between the freezers, they clapped him into the stockroom. Pretty soon everyone was showing their appreciation of what a little retouching could do. Everyone, that is, but me.

What had *really* happened? What did it mean, for me? Even if I could fix it, would Howard Powell still *want* me sailing with him? How would I feel if someone I'd invited out's dad had called me *"Mister* famous big-shot" and squirted window-cleaner? If I were him and he were me, would I ever speak to me again?

CHAPTER THIRTEEN

A Fiat. Two Escorts, a Skoda, a Pascoe's Pasties van, the Moorstock double-decker; a West Country Windows van, a Goad's Hill Cleansing Unit lorry, a Sierra, a Renault, a Saab – where *was* she? The traffic swashed by with no sign of M.

Four-forty already. M had promised she'd get back for Needham's. There was barely time to get there before "visitors out" at five.

At last I spotted the van. I waved. She pulled up. I jumped in.

"All right, then?"

"I suppose. Where *were* you?"

"Twenty minutes' queue for the bridge. Town centre's blue murder on a Saturday."

Blue murder. Murder wasn't blue. Murder was purple or red. Or yellow. I sat back and thought. I thought about the wink. For the hundredth time since dinner I ran through the morning's horrible happenings in my head. For the hundredth time I re-ran Howard Powell's parting wink.

Once again he cracked palms with Gwen. Once again he turned at the door. Once again he winked, for me and me alone. The wink was everything.

What did it mean? Had it been a see-you-next-Saturday wink? Or had it been a see-you-around-but-not-if-I-see-you-first kind of wink? Was Saturday on, or off? D had told him no in a way it was hard to forget. Was Howard Powell solid? If we turned up, would he have us?

I had to decide. I was on my way to Uncle Champion. Where would I ask him to take us – if he'd take us anywhere at all? Mount Hope or Cletchley Quay?

Suddenly I *did* decide. The wink was enough. I would try for the Quay at one-thirty. This time next week, Pinny would either be queen of the river, or high and dry on Cletchley Quay. It was a lot to gamble on the blink of an eye.

"Busy today?" asked M. "Fairly." I looked across. Her earrings bobbed on the collar of her going-to-town leather jacket. If I was going to, now was the time to tell her. She knew nothing at all – yet – about this morning. It was a chance to get in before D.

All I had to say was, Howard Powell asked me sailing but Dad won't let me, so can I? At first she'd be gobsmacked. Then she'd be star-struck, which was worse. Then she'd want to meet him. She'd insist on running me to Cletch-ley Quay, to meet him. Then I'd have to tell her I was taking Pinny. Then she'd stop me taking her. There was no way around it. Whatever D said – I had a feeling it wouldn't be much – I would say nothing.

"Get what you want?" I asked.

"No four-pack juice. No Thrifty Marg till next month. Everything else. Except six-pack yogurts and Prairiedog Crisps."

"No Prairiedogs?"

"Next month."

The run to Jackson's Wholesale, Tarmouth, was a regular monthly chore. Usually I had to help. But M was in sympathetic mode. Would I like Paul or Jamie to stay over if I didn't like a film? There were trainers I'd like in the market. Would I like a new pair of trainers? We'd moved on to things I might like for tea by the time we reached Redmoor.

By the green iron gates at Needham's she gave me the plan. There were just ten minutes to five.

"I got the old boy's socks he wanted in Dug-dale's. We'll run 'em up to him, say hello. Then we'll nip up the chippy. Ten minutes, all right?"

"But I want to see Mrs Pinder. I haven't seen

her since she came back from hospital."

"You got a hope. Tea-bell at five."

At four fifty-three I tore in the day lounge.
Catherine Cuthburt looked up.

"Mrs Pinder?" I asked wildly.

"I don't really know, I'm afraid." She carried on winding wool on a big pink ball,
unravelling a cardigan to knit into egg cosies
or something else no one could live without.

"Isn't that her in the garden?"

"Is it? I really couldn't tell you. Do you like
pink?"

Pinny was marooned on the lawn. I coughed
a bit, coming up behind her, to let her know I
was there.

"Pinny!"

"My dear life. Where've you been hidin'?"

"How are you? Feeling better?"

"Take me in, won't you, dear? I can't shift
me wheels on the grass. I never wanted no
garden in the first place."

"Why'd you come out?"

"Oh, well, if Catherine Cuthburt says you
got to 'ave fresh air, you got 'ave fresh air."

"Miss Cuthburt brought you out?"

"She brought me out, the snake – an' here
I've stopped. An' no beggar come to wheel me
in."

There wasn't time for all this. There was
only time to tell her. First I had to get her in. I
strained down on her wheelchair handles. It

took me all my strength to break the wheel lock she'd got in the grass. Finally I got her moving and rolled her slowly towards the path.

"Before we go in, I've got a surprise—" I began.

"Is that tea-bell? I'll go dinin' room, please, dear."

When we reached the patio I flipped on her brake and faced her.

"Pinny. Listen. You know your birthday next Saturday?"

"I got to get in. I'll miss me pasty. Birthday. Saturday. Yes, I b'lieve 'tis."

"Pinny, we're going up Mount Hope. Like I promised."

"Mount Hope? Up the old place?"

"Yes. We're going Saturday. Only you mustn't—"

"Shall I go, then? Shall I go Mount Hope?"

"But you mustn't tell anyone, because there'll be a fuss. All right? All you've got to do is be ready for half past one, next Saturday. And not tell anyone."

For a moment she forgot her tea. For a moment she forgot everything but the old place. It was a perfect moment. The old folk clattered in the dining room. The traffic buzzed by behind the wall. The clock in the day lounge ticked. It showed two minutes past five. I could catch Uncle Champion on the stairs.

I flipped off her brake and brought her

round. Elaine saw me struggling in the dining room door.

"Next Saturday," I whispered. "Half past one."

"We won't tell 'em, shall us?" hissed Pinny, catching my arm. "We won't tell 'em nothin' about it."

"That's right," I said, "we won't. Here's Elaine to get you."

I ran for the stairs. On my way through the empty day lounge I swiped up Catherine Cuthburt's big pink ball of wool off her chair. I took a good swing and buzzed it as far as I could through the open patio doors. It sailed off left in the bushes, unwinding as it went. Before its tail of yarn had settled, I was halfway up the stairs.

Uncle Champion was just coming out of his room. Lucky he was deaf. I wondered how often he missed tea-bell altogether.

"Uncle Jack, I—"

"Your mother's in the car. She says get on, she's waiting."

All the things I'd thought of to say went out of the window like Miss Cuthburt's ball of wool. I'd planned to play on his vanity. I'd planned to explain how *he* was the only one Mrs Pinder would ride with. How he was the only one who could take her – which he was – and how much she'd appreciate it – which she would. I'd planned to praise up his driving. If nothing else worked, I meant to use meeting Howard Powell as a lure.

Now, when it was needed, none of this would come. I didn't think anything at all would come, for a moment. Then something came – but it wasn't words. My face ran tears and a big lump burst in my chest.

Uncle Champion looked up the landing and down the stairs. He pushed back his door. "You come in wi' me," he said softly.

He steered me into his room. He sat me down on his bed.

"That's the ticket," he said. "You tell it your Uncle Champion. Your Uncle Champion'll see you right."

He sat down beside me while I dried my face with a tissue. When I was ready, I began.

CHAPTER
FOURTEEN

"... farming was different then. Early morning I'd go on the wagon with Father down the limekilns ... come back with steaming hot lime up behind. That was for spreading on the fields... We didn't go over to fruit like ... a lot did. Father wouldn't touch it. I used to say, when the farm was mine ... I'd go into fruit in a big way. See, I thought I'd ... come into the farm in time, but ... then we had dairy. I was ten when I started to milking. Father'd come out and watch over... Then two years later Father ... died and I had to carry on proper, until—"

Snap. Margaret Bath stopped the tape. Pretty boring stuff, except for the voice. It was an old man's voice, dragging out words as though words cost money. "Who is it?" I asked politely.

"One of my longest memories," said Margaret Bath. "Ninety-two and sound as a bell. I taped him Monday last."

On the shelf behind her were a stack of tape cassettes labelled for a dozen people's memories: "Mr Dingle, Ferryman"; "Ida Batey, Draper's Assistant"; "Hendra, R., Market Gardener"; "Jimmy Clemens, Miner"; "Mrs A. Pinder, flower picker"; "Miss P. Madaver, Schoolteacher"; "Bolitho, G., Churchwarden".

"You've got Mrs Pinder," I said.

"Want to hear her?"

"Um. Not just now."

"Mr Dingle's worth a listen. Some marvellous stories. I use them in my talks."

"Oh, yeh. 'A Life in the Valley'. I saw the poster."

"Last piece of flapjack? Going begging?"

"Thanks." Tea with Margaret Bath wasn't my first choice after a hard day's graft in the stockroom. As far as M was concerned it was tea at Paul Doney's, and somehow I couldn't help wishing it was. But I'd put her off once already. Besides, there were things I wanted to ask her. And I was curious. What would her cottage be like?

What it was like was a car-boot sale in a greenhouse. Make that a phone box. There was hardly room to scratch. Over the shelf with the tapes was another crammed with books, and over that another, glinting old glass bottles.

Round the tops of the walls were rows of plates with corn dollies and feathers and stuff between. The stairs in the corner were chocked solid with pots of dried flowers and horny great shells and wild-looking plants. It was a wonder she could climb them.

There were string things trailing plants from the ceiling, and urn things sprouting plants up to meet them. The mantelpiece and the window-sill and the piano were all over jars and rocks and driftwood, with a Chinese fan and a ram's skull with horns in pride of place. If she'd lived in the cottage when the cottage was new, they'd have hauled her out for a witch.

I was sharing my corner with a giant cactus in a chamber pot and a psychedelic milk churn filled with teasels and peculiar walking sticks. Everything that wasn't covered in anything else had trays of seedlings. There was just about room for the table, and us.

"One thing," I said. "Why were you up Mount Hope?"

"When was that?"

"Oh. A while back, now."

"Well, it's where Mrs Pinder used to live. I wanted to see it."

"So did I. And I'm taking her on a mystery tour on Saturday and we're stopping by Mount Hope on the way – it's her birthday Saturday, and she's mad to see it again…"

"I know she is. You know Mount Hope belongs to Howard Powell?"

"It's him that's taking us. We're going down the river to Morden Quay and – d'you think it's all right, Morden Quay?"

"Why shouldn't it be?"

"Because of, you know, Mr William. Being shot there. She was on about it the day she took off from Needham's. I got her these flowers – she was crying an' stuff…"

Margaret Bath sighed. "Yes," she said, "I know. But going to Morden Quay's the best thing you could do."

"It is?"

"I think she needs to see the old places again before she – well, it's a good thing to do."

It was a good thing to hear her say it. Why did Howard Powell have to moor at Morden Quay of all places? I hadn't thought it through, at the time. But ever since I'd fixed it with Uncle Champion I'd wished it were anywhere else.

I finished up the flapjack. I drank my tea. Margaret Bath drank hers. So she was worried about Pinny. So was I, what else? Then I remembered the picture.

"What about the picture? You said you'd let me see it."

"Oh. *The Last Field*. It's in my studio."

She got up to show me. I dodged the giant cactus and the teasels and the churn and the piano and I followed her out across the slate-flagged passage.

She turned at the door. "What time will you be at Morden?"

"I'm not sure."

"About what time, d'you think?"

"I suppose … leave at two … 'bout four, I suppose."

She nodded, and thought a moment. Then she opened the studio door.

Margaret Bath's studio was almost completely empty, by way of a change. It was a big room filled with light. On a splatter-mat in the centre stood her easel with a half-finished painting. The only other things were a chair with a hat and a hot-water bottle, and a work-bench jumbled over in artists' stuff, plus a bowl of fruit; and canvases, some empty, some not, loosely stacked along the wall.

She lifted down the half-finished painting. It was going to be a morning mist in the valley, with a red sun breaking over.

"I'm moving away from landscapes into portraits. I haven't had much time to finish things off lately, what with Stopeley—"

"Is it done, then? The painting of Stopeley?"

"It's done. I don't know if it's hung."

I hoped it was. I hoped it was hung and Black William gone from his Kennel. I hoped he was eating dust in the attic, with nothing to stare out but the water cistern.

I spotted *The Last Field* against the far wall. It had an old brown photo taped to its top edge. The photo showed a laughing girl on a narrow ladder in a tree. She had a long dark dress and long dark hair, and the tree held the ladder, and the ladder held her, and she held her basket. And laughed. What was she picking? Cherries, I supposed.

The painting beneath took me back to the field, bright with a thousand flowers. They would be blown and papery now. But Margaret Bath had made them blaze for as long as anyone had a wall to hang a picture on.

I could see what she'd done. It was very clever. She'd licked in the details and sharpened the foreground. And just left of centre she was adding a flower picker, a girl – the girl on the ladder.

"I think she'll fit, don't you?" asked Margaret Bath.

"Is it… ?"

"Addie Hand. The last flower picker."

The face in the photo was Pinny, but not Pinny. I could just about see it. The eyes, the set of the face. The laugh. It was Pinny as a girl who climbed ladders, picked cherries, and laughed when she dropped them when the photographer came round.

"Weird, isn't it?" I said. "Seeing someone young you've only seen old."

"Yes," she said, "I know what you mean.

Look around if you want. I'll put the kettle on."

"Again?"

"Again."

I flipped through the paintings stacked against the wall. Some were paintings of places I knew. Leigh Rock. Cap Hill. The chapel at the Saint's Quay. Best of all were the views of the Valley.

Then there were voices, outside on the path:

"I'll pick you up on me way back. About an hour."

"Don't go ... to any trouble. I can ... walk if I have to."

"Ninety-two, an' he can walk if he has to. You're not walking. I said, you're not – are you all right to go in? I said, are you all right to go in?"

"I'm ... all right, now. Thank you."

"Well, then. About an hour."

I knew that slow voice. I'd heard it before, sometime not long ago – when? And where was Margaret Bath? What was she doing? Filling the kettle from a well?

I whipped up the corridor and checked a dim kitchen: a Rayburn, herbs and pots and wooden ladles hanging down like – like stuff like that does, and no Margaret Bath. "Hello?" I called, "Hello?" I checked the kettle. The kettle was hot. Where could she...

Then he was knocking. Knocking once,

twice, on Margaret Bath's front door. And waiting. And knocking again. Might as well see what he wanted.

I went down the passage. I opened the white wooden door.

"Yes?"

He was an old, old, *old* man. Once he'd been tall. Now he had a lifetime on his back he was just bent. He had watery blue eyes and deep furrows in his face either side of his nose.

"Yes?" I said again.

"Miz Bath ... at home?"

"She is, yes. Um. I'll just get her."

"I'm ... expected."

Got it. It was the voice on the tape. It was the old bloater I'd heard not half an hour since, maundering on about his father's farm. Ninety-two. No wonder he looked old.

"Who shall I tell her?"

"Tell what?"

"What name, I mean."

"My name? My name – " he said – "my name is ... Harry Start."

CHAPTER
FIFTEEN

"Ah," said Margaret Bath, "I see you've met." She plumped down a basket of washing behind the kitchen door.

"Where were you? I didn't know where you were," I said, not making much sense. It was obvious she'd been up the garden picking in washing while the kettle boiled.

"Come in, Harry. This is—"

"Graham," I put in quickly.

She gave me a funny look. "Graham's a friend of Mrs Pinder. The Mrs Pinder we were talking about last Monday—"

"Don't want to talk about that," said Harry Start shortly.

"Harry's come to let me sketch him, haven't you, Harry?"

"How did you – how d'you know each other?" I asked.

"Harry came to my little talk the other week. Afterwards, he was telling me about point stuff."

"Point stuff?"

"See, you'd get … point stuff off of the Point…" started Harry, none too clearly.

"Harry's told me a lot about farming in the Valley. As well as lime, they used to use dead leaves as fertilizer. The leaves'd build up in big banks off Medlin Point. They'd barge them upriver and use them to spread on the fields. Point stuff, they called it."

"Better not tell … what else we used," said Harry Start. "Not if we're … havin' tea. Hur, hur. Hur."

He looked at us like a dog that aims to please. "Hur, hur." It was his idea of a joke.

How long could this go on? We were talking fertilizer with the man who'd blown away the Flower King. I hadn't got over Harry Start, not in a million years. I sneaked a look in his wishy-washy eye. He looked back dimly. He was just an old man. He had about as much to do with Harry Start, murderer, as Pinny had with the laughing girl on the ladder.

Margaret Bath smiled. "Shall we go through?"

We went through. We had cake, and more tea. At least, Harry Start had cake and tea. He didn't mind … if he did. He was … partial to a bit of cake, thank you. Margaret Bath brought out her sketch-pad. She made some opening swipes with her charcoal. For a while, there was nothing but the sound of her sweeping stick on the page.

Harry Start had finished his cake. He looked around a bit. He edged away from the cactus. He fiddled with his sleeve.

The charcoal scratching stopped. "Harry – could you – that's it, straight ahead. Look at Graham, would you?"

He fixed me with his dead fish eyes. "Not bad ... weather we're havin' for..."

"How about Mini Masterbrain?" I fished it out of my pocket. Anything to keep him still, except look in those empty eyes.

I showed him the coloured pegs. "You put them in your end of the board, here – and don't show me. Then I have to work out the colours."

He fumbled the pegs while I looked away. I turned back. I put in a first line. Blue, green, orange, yellow.

"Right, see these?" I showed him the black and whites. "If one of my colours is in the right place, you put in a black peg, here. If it's the right colour, but in the wrong place, you put in a white peg instead."

"How's that again?"

I showed him again. Margaret Bath looked up, looked down. Her charcoal scratched and whorled.

Blue, green, orange, yellow. Harry Start looked and thought. I thought I'd grow old myself before he made a move. But at last he pinched up a peg. He dropped it, and pinched up another. He tried to put it in, and almost upset the board. He tried again. He pulled back his hand. One black peg, was all.

"So," I said carefully, "I've got one right colour, and it's in the right place. And that's all."

He nodded slowly.

One colour right, three colours wrong. But there were only six colours in all. There had to be at least one white peg as well. Even repeating one peg at random as the one in the right place, there were only two colours left to try. Not enough to make a fresh line – unless he'd made a mistake.

What did I expect? The silly old kipper was giving me the wrong information. I'd show him up on the next line. I put in red, green, brown – then what? Blue. Red, green, brown, blue. What would he make of that?

I watched his fumbling hands and despised him. This was the man for wrong information. Acting on what an eight-year-old girl had told him, he'd shot down an innocent man. He wasn't sorry. He was having tea and cake, thank you very much. He was ninety-two, and the Flower King wasn't.

He brought back his hand and looked smug.

Two white pegs. Two colours right, but none in the right place. But now I didn't trust him.

I whipped in another line angrily. Orange, brown, blue, yellow. Tricky, friendly, sorry, hopeful. Eat *that*!

Slowly he fumbled one black peg. Slowly he pushed it in. I waited. He waited. He looked up. He was enjoying himself now.

"You got ... the wrong idea, boy."

"No," I said coldly. "You're telling me wrong. There's got to be more right than that. There's only six colours."

Margaret Bath looked up at me a moment. Then she bent over her pad.

"Think on, boy," he said. "Think on. Hur, hur. Hur."

His watery not-sorry eyes knew something I didn't. Suddenly I felt like throwing the board in his face. I snatched it up. "Let me see what you've got."

I looked in the end he'd been hiding. Red, blue, red, blue. Angry, sorry, angry, sorry. Only two colours in all. No wonder I couldn't get it. He'd been playing two-colour doubles all along, when I hadn't told him doubles.

"That's doubles," I said, jumping up. "I never said doubles. You should've used four colours different."

"Can't help that, boy," he said, not sorry at all. "Can't help it if you had ... the wrong idea."

"No," I shouted, really angry now, "YOU had the wrong idea. You went and shot the wrong man."

Margaret Bath dropped her charcoal. Harry Start stood up. His arms shook. His mouth flapped.

"I was on'y sixteen, I din' know ... what I was doing. I never would've done nothin', but for—"

"Graham," said Margaret Bath, "I think that'll do."

"But you did, didn't you?" I shouted, ignoring her. "You asked the wrong thing and you DID the wrong thing, and my friend Mrs Pinder thinks it's HER fault cos she told you, and you never should've done it ANYWAY. He was only loading flowers, AND YOU SHOT HIM."

Suddenly I flipped. I caught up the tray of little coloured pegs and I flung them on Harry Start.

A hundred plastic pegs in green and blue and red and yellow and brown and orange and black and white showered down on Harry Start. They pinged off his head and stuck in his collar and dropped in his tea. They jumped on the table, they jumped on the cactus, they jumped on Margaret Bath's sketch-pad and they jumped on Margaret Bath.

A hundred coloured pegs, rattling down on jars and shells and pots and plants and urns and seedlings, like a sick-in-bed hot cross nightmare, rattling and falling and jumping in a hundred separate places.

CHAPTER
SIXTEEN

It was a quiet week, the week after Margaret Bath's. I didn't feel much like King of the World. In fact, I felt pretty bad.

Tuesday, I found a new pair of trainers on my bed. At first I thought they were Bar-Tok's, but they weren't. They were just a cheesy clone. Air-flo soles, but the trim was wrong. I didn't go to Club on Wednesday. I didn't go anywhere at all. The most I did was avoid D. Avoiding D was easy. He was framing up for exchange of contract on Pollock's, and he couldn't see anything else. M was more of a problem. She even asked me if there was anything I'd like to talk to her about. As if.

At least there was something to look forward to. Big Saturday was just round the corner. I pictured Pinny at Cletchley Quay. Pinny meeting Howard Powell. Riding the

Avatar. Coming home to Mount Hope. Having tea at Stopeley Rise. Big Saturday would wipe the slate clean.

Thursday, I finished my Energy Project. Glaze U Rite replaced the plate glass window at the stores. I thought about ringing Margaret Bath. I almost did. But what could I say? Sorry I threw a wobbler at your place on Monday? What would *she* say? She was probably still picking Masterbrain pegs out of the pot plants.

As I said, it was quiet. Then, Friday, something terrible happened. It started with bumps in the night. Or rather, pings in the night.

I woke without knowing what had woken me. *Ting, ting. Ping.* I flipped on the light. Eleven-fifty. *Ting, ping. Ting.* It was something outside, something – tinny. Something tinny out the back. I trailed through to the bathroom and opened the window on the back garden.

The night was filled with sparks. What the pinging was, was spiteful little fiery sparks falling out of the sky on the corrugated iron roof of the shed. The shed roof was hopping. I looked up. A giant plume of orange sparks was fanning up in the night sky, torn by the wind from – from where?

D hustled in behind me in his disgusting striped pyjamas. He craned left out of the window.

"What is it?" I asked, a bit freaked.

"Search me," he mumbled, looking. "Looks like somethin's on fire."

"Let me see." I looked again. The wind woofed. A blast of brilliant sparks pressed over the shed and fired the night sky like November the fifth. Little crackling bits of half-burned stuff came end over end in the garden.

"There must be a fire up the road. Wow! Wonder where it is?" I pulled in my head. D had disappeared.

I looked out again, looked back. D was tearing on a sweater on the landing.

"Where are you going?"

"Up the road to take a look," said D, fixing his flies on the stairs.

"Wait – " I said. "I'm coming."

I flung myself down to the door. I jammed on a coat and wellies. I wasn't about to miss *this*.

We stumped along Top Road in silence. We weren't the only ones. We crested the rise that was really just a ripple in the back of Cap Hill along with several others. Now we could see it. The fire was big, all right.

There wasn't much smoke. Just a brilliant heart of orange, feeding the plume in the sky, the giant plume of sparks. Now I could hear it. I could hear it tearing and crackling, and over it – shouting, a siren, more shouts. It was somewhere down left, horribly close to...

"Mount Hope, it looks like," said D. "Or Pike's place. Big old fire, isn' it?"

"Is it Mount Hope? It's not Mount Hope, is it?" I bleated.

"Looks like," said D, pushing on. Dave Pascoe pushed on with us as we came by his gate.

"Aw'right then, Dave?" nodded D. "Some blaze!"

"Yep," said Dave. "Dennis got supper well-done tonight." That was Dennis Pike, he meant.

Let it be Pike's place, I wished as I went. Let it be Lower Hope. Please.

"Hope it in't Pike's," said D. "Tin't Pikey's, is it?"

Now we could see the engines. One ahead on the hard shoulder lit up like a Christmas tree, another at right angles in the gravel depot. Running figures flashed across the lights, ducking and dodging, running and running.

We reached the top of Toy's Lane – or rather, the place where the top of Toy's Lane used to be. Now it was a mess of cables and hoses, mud and metal connectors. *Klup.* Someone flipped up the metal cover at the foot of the fire hydrant by D's leg. Someone else rapidly unscrewed something inside.

A couple of grim-looking firemen passed us in the lane, their stiff waterproof arms

171

zwipping against their bodies as they went, the light from the engine up top flashing them all the shades of panic. It was a lot of firemen for an empty old cottage. Why would they pull out all the stops to save Mount Hope?

For it *was* Mount Hope. Any hope it wasn't was choked by the roaring walls and lintels streaming fire in the sky where once Pinny'd aired her sheets. We were just in time for the roof. With a shrug like thunder it caved and broke. A terrible flame rolled up the spark-plume. Everyone but the firemen drew back.

The hoses searched the corner nearest Lower Hope. A couple more played on Lower Hope itself, swashing the roof clear of sparks. The firemen weren't fighting to save Mount Hope at all. The fight for Mount Hope was lost already. Mount Hope could burn, providing it burned alone. They were fighting to prevent a flashover to lived-in Lower Hope.

After a while I made out the Pikes huddled in the hedge. Mr and Mrs and Sean, at least. D headed over, nosing for juicy details and making out he wasn't, like everyone else in the crowd. How did it start? It never! You smelt somethin' around eight? Get out. Must've been smoulderin' prob'ly.

Where was Sonia Pike? At last I spotted her, a little way apart. Her face flashed orange as she watched. Suddenly she felt me looking. She glanced over once, quickly. She changed the

172

way she was standing a couple of times. Then she looked steadily in the fire, as though she hadn't seen me at all. She looked as guilty as a fat rat in a cake-shop window.

I snuck up beside her. I waited. "So what did you do?"

She looked in the fire. The fire crashed. "Didn't do nothin'."

What was it Dave Pascoe had said? Dennis Pike got his supper well-done tonight. Something was cooking, all right. But it wasn't Pikey's supper.

"That range – " I started idly, as if I never meant to finish – "that range never was no good."

"No, he never—"

"Never what?"

"Never … lit prop'ly."

"You lit it and it went out?"

"On'y a few sticks. I was playin' bird's-nest soup. I did a few sticks but he never caught, so I—"

"You put sticks in the firebox and lit them? And let it go?"

Sonia Pike shrugged. "It was jus' a bit of smoke. It never caught nor nothin'."

"When was that?"

"'Bout seven. Jus' a wincy bit of smoke, that's all."

"So it smouldered since seven and broke out the back of the firebox up the wall—"

"I 'spect it was that old nest," said Sonia Pike carelessly. "That ole bird's nest I was cookin' in the oven."

I looked at Sonia Pike with loathing. She'd cooked *my* goose with her bird's-nest soup. What would happen now, with a howling black hole in Big Saturday where Mount Hope used to be?

The fire was lopsided now. The firemen were winning. Lower Hope would survive, with its tacky plastic windows and extension intact. Sonia Pike would survive with her stupid head intact, unless I—

"If you say anythin'," she went on smoothly, "I'll say it was *your* idea. An' Sean'll say it, too."

I opened my mouth and closed it again. Horrible, horrible, horrible. It was me who'd put bird's-nest soup in her head. Any whisper, any suspicion of more trouble and I could file joy under never.

"Show's over," said D, looming up next to me. "Let's clear off 'ome."

Now that there was no danger to life or limb and nothing else burning down, D was ready to go. I was ready to go myself. Everything bad that *could* happen had happened already.

Our wellies hit the same rhythm coming back over the rise. It was strange to be out in the dark with D. It was strange to be out with D at all. I looked back over my shoulder. The glow in the sky had faded. So had any idea of bringing Pinny to Mount Hope – or what *had* been Mount Hope, and was now a heap of hissing timbers over a sad and twisted range.

"Good blaze, wan't it?" said D. I walked on. I didn't feel like talking.

He tried again. "You can go sailin' tomorrow with fancypants if you want."

"Thanks," I said coolly. "I'm going anyway." He thought about this for a bit. When we reached the front gate he fumbled in his pocket. "Twenty quid," he huffed in my face, finding my hand with his, pressing my shoulder with the other. "Buy yourself somethin'."

"What for?"

"Take it. Get yourself somethin' you want." He found my eyes in the dark. "Be a good kid."

I saw in that moment he really couldn't cope. He couldn't cope at all. It was the only thing he could think of to do. The only way D knew to try and make things right.

CHAPTER SEVENTEEN

"I'm off now," I shouted, hoping M hadn't heard.

But she had. "Wait. I'll run you down."

It's true what they say. Things *do* look better in the morning. It was Big Saturday. So Mount Hope was up in smoke – wasn't there still the *Avatar* and tea at Stopeley Rise? I didn't know quite how I'd play it with Pinny, but I was beginning to see things had a way of working out all by themselves if you let them. Pity M didn't see it. Now she was angling to meet Howard Powell, just like I'd known she would. It was D's fault. If D had told her nothing it would be too much.

"No, he – he wouldn't like that. He doesn't like meeting people."

"Get out. Give me a chance to smooth things over."

"It won't matter about that—"

"What you wearin' them scruffy old trainers for? Where's the new ones I got you up the market?"

I opened the front door. I slipped round it. "I'm – saving them. They'll only get wet."

M clapped her pockets for car keys. She rummaged in her coat. "Funny. Had 'em here this morning—"

"I'm cycling down and Howard Powell's dropping me back," I gabbled. "Can you record *Nightwatch*, seven o'clock on Two – thanks, see you."

"Wait, I got 'em here somewhere—"

But I was out and clean away. I swung on the bike I'd primed earlier by the kerb and hit out for Lower Cletchley before M could reach the door.

"Wait a minute, will you?" she screamed behind me. "I said WAIT!"

"CLETCHLEY QUAY 2" said the signpost labelling Under Road. But I wasn't going to Cletchley Quay – not yet, at least. I took the first right off Under Road and power-pedalled back up the hill. Just when I thought I never would, I reached Sandman's Corner. I was up on Top Road again, a couple of hundred metres from the point where I'd started. I checked Big Saturday Countdown on my watch. Exactly one-fifteen. I was on schedule. I could only hope Uncle Champion was, too.

I'd need all the help I could get to smuggle Pinny out of Needham's.

I took a long, cool tug on my water bottle – Citrus Zing and Sportzade, mixed. I checked the road for M. Perhaps the back of the cutlery drawer hadn't been such a good idea. Funny how you can have a whole room to hide a set of car keys in and not see where to hide them.

I checked my clothes. I had on my favourite cowpat-green sweater. Nothing special, but I liked the feel. It felt trusty. A trusty old sweater. I checked my hair. No stress.

Suddenly I felt that everything was as right as it would ever be. Some things happened, other things didn't. I was moving through all of it on a course of my own.

A gap in the traffic opened in front of me. I turned the bike for Needham's Green, and Pinny.

Uncle Champion's old black Morris was waiting outside Needham's, shiny as a beetle and ready to roll. Cool, I thought. Good old Unc. Then I wondered how things were going on inside.

I chained up the bike and snuck in the side door. The giant washing-machine in the laundry room ticked nastily during a break in its routine. It was thinking what to do next. Just as it started its rinse cycle I heard Uncle Champion smarming in the kitchen.

"Ladies. We can't have this. You got to put your feet up after dinner."

"Get away, Jack," – Mrs Screech's voice. "Dishes won't do themselves, will they, Jan?"

No answer from Jan. Then Uncle Champion again: "You don't want to go puttin' they lovely white hands in that dish-wash muck."

"Flattery don't butter no bread," honked Janet, like the stiff she was.

"Dining room's to clear, Jan." Mrs Screech again.

Uncle Champion rallied. "They old plates'll wait. Old Jack's got a treat for his best girls."

I grinned. Uncle Jack was in overdrive. I pictured the fusty great box of chocs he was flashing them. I had to hand it to him. He was taking care of the brain police the only way he knew how – with flattery. He was flattering them senseless, and they were falling for it, hook, line and sinker.

"You soft thing, Jack. You're spoiling us."

"And who's to spoil you if I don't? Here's for Janet."

"Oh. Well, now. It's not often you get a – well, it's not often."

"You take the weight off your feet a minute. You ladies got to take care of yourselves."

I slipped through into the hall. The coast was clear. Of course it was. Uncle Champion had seen to that. Now it was up to me to find Pinny and get her out. But Uncle Jack had seen to that as well.

Elaine was waiting by the day room door. "Here's her things." She handed me Pinny's coat and bag. "Two Mitocaine tablets if she fusses. They're in her bag. Keep her warm and don't be too late back."

For a moment I felt confused. "Does – does she know then? Mrs Screech?"

"You're joking. She'll know when she reads your uncle's note. Hurry, or we'll never get her out."

I ran the coat and bag to the car. Together we fetched Pinny from the dining room, for all the world as though it were time for her afternoon nap. She looked up. Two spots of colour stood in her cheeks. I felt like the worst kind of traitor. Not only wasn't I taking her where I said I'd take her, but the place I said I'd take her wasn't even *there* any more. How could I tell her? Somehow it felt like my fault Mount Hope had burned out. *And* there was Harry Start to tell about – or not. But I didn't want to think about that.

"Elaine give me a lovely scarf for me birthday, din' you, dear? I had bedsocks off'f Screech, and Jack Champion give me fudge."

Pinny eyed me shrewdly. I had nothing. Nothing at all to give, but the homecoming-that-wasn't.

I spread my arms. "Ready for a birthday mystery tour?"

Together we got her wheelchair down the front ramp to Uncle Champion's car. There was a sticky moment when I realized she'd need the wheelchair with her. But Elaine was one step ahead. Already she was loading a walking frame in the back. I watched her gratefully.

"Thanks, Elaine."

She smiled. She had a nice smile. "Do her the world of good to get out, if you're careful. She'll go best in the back, don't you think?"

I did think. Carefully we edged Pinny out of her chair. She managed a step or two to the car. Then we brought her round, backside first, and braced an arm each to lower her in. Once in, she was set to go.

"Where's the driver to? Can't go nowhere without no driver."

"Can you stay a minute?" I asked Elaine. "I'll just get Uncle Champion."

I flashed through the hall with my heart pounding. Where was he? Still in the kitchen? Couldn't be. I peeped in the day room. No joy. Perhaps he was fussing in his room. I pounded up the stairs and burst in. No Uncle Jack. I hammered down again and listened by the kitchen door.

"Have a coffee cream, Jan."

"Don't mind if I do. What's got into the old boy today?"

"Mus' be wanting something, Jan. You

better watch yourself."

Whispering and cackling. More cackling. Mrs Screech and Janet were well away. I only wished we were. Where *was* he? Any moment now things would go wrong. The front door was flapping. I dashed wildly through it.

Uncle Jack was in the car. The engine was running. Pinny sat expectantly behind him, eyes front. I flung myself in beside him.

"All right then, boy?" he winked. He found first gear. The car jumped. We ground up the hill in second.

"Where were you?"

"Nipped out the side," he said. "Went smooth as glass, din' it?"

"It was – " but I couldn't think what it was. "It was *so* tidy, Uncle Jack. Like—"

"Like John Gently," he said. " 'Twas clever, like John Gently'd do. All right there, Mrs P.?"

"Lovely, thank you, Jack. It's a lovely ride thank you."

We signalled left and pulled on Fore Street. "MOORSTOCK 10 CLETCHLEY 3" said the post by the lights. We pulled away on amber.

I looked round. Pinny's face said it all. Big Saturday was on wheels at last.

CHAPTER
EIGHTEEN

"Here he comes," I whispered quickly. "He calls me Graham, but don't worry about it."

One-fifty, exactly. Cletchley Quay was busy, in a sleepy, lunchtime, don't-do-today-what-you-can-put-off-till-tomorrow sort of way. The *Avatar* rode lazily by the wooden pier. A few other craft bobbed round her like ducks round a swan. Along the bank a bit, the brothers Nash were eel-fishing with bits of bacon. A rancid chip paper blew against my legs. I kicked it off. It blew in the side of the gull-splashed bench and stuck.

Howard Powell hurried to meet us. He was in full Jolly Sailor mode.

"Graham! Glad you could make it!" He didn't seem a bit surprised.

"This is my Uncle Champion," I said. "He brought us. And this is Mrs Pinder."

He took her hand like a gallant. "Mrs Pinder. Graham's told me so much about you. But may I call you Pinny?"

"Call me a doorstop, I won't be no different," teased Pinny.

I loved her for it. She was what she was, even meeting Howard Powell. She would never pretend to be something she wasn't.

"Ah," smiled Howard Powell. "A rose by any other name."

She twinkled back. They were losing me, but they seemed to understand one another.

"'Twasn't so much roses as daffs, was it, Ad?" said Uncle Champion suddenly. "Mrs P. picked Valley flowers, you know."

Howard Powell closed his eyes and put on his Actor Voice:

"For oft, when on my couch I lie
In vacant or in pensive mood,
They flash upon that inward eye
Which is the bliss of solitude;"

"And then my heart with pleasure fills, and dances with the daffodils," finished Uncle Jack triumphantly. It was the end of the daffodils poem he loved so much.

Howard Powell smiled. Uncle Champion smiled. Janie Powell smiled. Janie. She hadn't said a word. I'd hardly noticed she was there.

"This is Janie," I told Pinny. "Mr Powell's

daughter. She's down for the holidays."

"Hello, dear," said Pinny – but her eyes were on the *Avatar*.

Why wouldn't they be? She outshone every craft in sight. There wasn't one to touch her. Gleaming white, she flattered the river, the sky and the wooded hills beyond. The river was made for her.

"Well," said Howard Powell, "what are we waiting for? Pinny – may I hand you in?"

"Oh, my. On the boat?"

"On the boat. This," said Howard Powell proudly, "is the *Ava*. A lady in a million."

Uncle Champion waved us off. He grew smaller and smaller with every lick of the wind. I was glad I'd had a moment to thank him.

"Thanks, Uncle Jack." I squeezed his hand. "I couldn't have done it without you."

"Couldn't have done it without *you*, boy," he said. "I an't had courage enough to drive out Cletchley way in years."

I waved him smaller and smaller. Then the *Avatar* took the viaduct turn and Uncle Champion was gone.

Pinny had taken the cabin-roof seat because I'd wanted her to. Howard Powell sat opposite at the helm, and I sat beside him, watching Pinny's face as the sheets slapped above and the river rolled away on either side. It was a perfect day. We were making a lazy three or four knots under half-sail only. Even so, it was fresh. Pinny pulled down her hat. I jumped up and tucked in the bottom of the blanket Howard Powell had wrapped round her.

"Graham tells me you knew the Flower King," started Howard Powell when I wished he wouldn't.

"Knew 'un well," said Pinny. I watched her anxiously.

"And did you know Mr William the Elder as well?"

"Mother boiled sheets for 'un. He was a nasty piece o' work."

"He didn't survive his son long, I believe."

"No," said Pinny grimly. "He 'ad his comeuppance that one."

"You never said," I said. "What happened?"

She fretted her hands on her blanket. But it was too late to turn the conversation now. Besides, if Black William had got his comeuppance, I wanted to know all about it.

" 'Twas just about a year after – after young Mr William."

"That'd be … nineteen-sixteen," put in Howard Powell, wheeling the helm to starboard.

"Mr Bowhays was out with the bailiffs a stormy night in March," said Pinny. "The wind was blowin' somethin' wild. I remember I said to Mother that night, I said be lucky if we got a roof over our 'eads come morning."

"And?" I asked.

"An' that's all about it. Storm come up on Clinker's Row, cuffed off a roof tile on Mr Bowhays' head."

"Clinker's Row? Down by the pottery?"

"The pottery, yes. The bone-works as was."

"And he was turning someone out when it happened?"

"He was down with the bailiffs, yes, watchin' the turn-out. Evictions was two a penny, them days. Bosinneys, it was. Six kiddies an' a baby. D'rectly the wind come up an' – *bang* – down goes Mr Bowhays with a roof tile in his 'ead. An' they fetch Doctor Prentice directly, an' Doctor Prentice says he's stone dead, straight off. Mr Bosinney – he worked over to Dingle's Shaft – Mr Bosinney said, times he'd asked Mr Bowhays to do somethin' about that roof. But he never would, see? He never would do nothin'."

She leaned back, tired, against her blankets.

I liked it. Killed by a falling roof tile off one of his own badly-maintained properties. I liked Black William's comeuppance a lot more than he had.

"Look," pointed Howard Powell. "Pentacote."

The big old manor house loomed in the trees, half a castle high and twice as wide. Its mullioned windows shone black in its grey stack walls. We stole beneath its little riverside chapel like a ship of thieves.

"If you'd told me – " said Pinny – "if you'd told me I'd be eighty-five an' sailin' by Pentacote, I'd've said get out, I never will."

"And here you are," I said, pleased that she was pleased.

"Eighty-five, an' here I am." She shook her head, believing it.

She looked around from side to side. The meadows opposite Pentacote ran every shade of green to the river's edge, spotted across with black and white Friesians dopy with sweet spring grass. It was all as I'd pictured it would be.

Her eyes caught mine. " 'Andsome, in't it, me bucky?" Did she say it, or think it? Anyway, it was. It was handsome, every bit.

Howard Powell cleared his throat. He'd been quieter than I'd ever known him. Perhaps he'd been minding the river. Or his own business, one or the other.

"Did you know Queen Victoria came here?" he asked. "Apparently she visited Pentacote in eighteen fifty-six. With the Prince Consort and the Princess Royal."

If she did, I thought, she could hardly have been more queenly than Pinny. But the trees had closed on Pentacote already. Already the strawberry slopes beyond were opening in front of us.

"Graham. Ask Janie if she wants the helm, would you?"

"Sure."

Janie Powell was up in the bows, as usual. I scrambled up beside her. Something had been bothering me a while. Suddenly I remembered what it was.

"Hey, where's Mrs Teagarden? I thought she was coming too."

Janie Powell turned me a dippy smile. "That's the best thing ever. Can you believe it, she's gone!"

"Gone where?"

"Mrs Teagarden," said Janie, "our darling Gaye, has taken herself off to her mother's."

"Since when?"

"Since last night. Dad got a call about ten-thirty saying Mount Hope was on fire – did you know? – and anyway, they had the most *enormous* row after, I know because I listened on the stairs. She said her mother'd never stand it ... Dad was hopeless ... she wouldn't stay at Stopeley a moment longer if he didn't get her mother somewhere civilized – and Dad called her a ... well, Dad called her a taxi, and it came and she went. Isn't it ecstasy?"

Janie Powell was pleased like I'd never seen her. Everyone was pleased. Except, perhaps, Howard Powell. Maybe he wasn't so pleased. Only yesterday Mount Hope had been his, and today it wasn't. Maybe that was why he was quiet. If he was quiet, I was glad. The last thing I needed was the fire at Mount Hope. For the moment I was safe. But I had to be sure.

"Can you not talk about Mount Hope in front of Pinny?" I asked. "Only, she doesn't know it's burned out yet, and I don't know how to tell her."

"I understand," said Janie Powell, as if she did. Whatever the change was, I liked it. Janie Powell was different altogether. I tried for a colour, but nothing came.

We sat and watched the *Avatar* pleating the river with her clean and nifty nose. The water curled away on either side and rocked the banks with a brimming, foamy fan that spread and died behind us as we went.

I fixed a spot and watched the foam. It wasn't really white. I didn't know *what* colour it was. I didn't know about colours any more. Pinny and Howard Powell talked dimly astern. The river hissed by. It couldn't be long now. The next bend, or the one after that. In a moment the limekilns would finger Morden Quay. I watched the foam and wished they wouldn't. I wished they'd stay round the next bend forever. I watched, and I didn't know what colour the foam was, and I didn't care at all.

Suddenly I remembered. "Oh. Your dad said d'you want to take the helm?"

"Bit late now," said Janie, "we're coming in."

The woods fell away as we tacked wide to

port on the bend. The Morden limekilns stared down like a skull. As we brought in the mainsail I saw the figures. Two figures – one tall and straight, one old and bent – waiting like sailors' wives for their ship to come in.

We wheeled in close and I looked again. I took up the mooring rope fiercely. One straight, one bent. When she saw me looking, she waved. Why had she done it? I braced my foot on the cleats till it hurt. Margaret Bath and Harry Start, all alone on Morden Quay. I didn't need to look again. I knew she was waving and waving.

CHAPTER NINETEEN

My first thought was Pinny. I had to prepare her. It would all be too much.

Already Howard Powell was whipping off her blankets. Already Margaret Bath was chivvying her up, a shaky step at a time, on the quay. Janie Powell hopped up after. That left me and the walking frame – and all the explanations in the world wouldn't fix Harry Start and his stupid bunch of stupid flowers, hanging on Margaret Bath's left shoulder like a freak show.

"You looked so fine coming round the bend," said Margaret Bath. "Didn't they, Harry?"

"Should've seen Pentacote," said Pinny. "We come under Pentacote like a dream, din' we, Howard?"

"That we did," said Howard Powell. "A following wind and the best of company – who could ask for more?"

I passed up the walking frame to Pinny. Margaret Bath settled her steady with a practised hand. Then she stepped back.

"Addie. This is Harry. Harry I was telling you about."

"I ... hope you don' mind, but I ... brought you these."

Poor old Harry Start was shaking like a stick, and his daffodils shook with him. What would Pinny think? Harry Start – after all this time – Harry Start, as changed as she was. What would she say?

But all she said was, "Harry, is it?"

But she watched – and I watched her, watching. She watched for the boy who'd crept up on her in the flower fields that morning seventy-seven years ago – the boy who'd asked her the question she'd answered over a thousand times since. "Yes," she could have said, "yes, that's Mr William – Mr William *the Younger*. Mr William the Elder's up the house." But she hadn't.

She hadn't, and that was why we were all there on Morden Quay seventy-seven years later – because of the answer, and the question that framed it.

Then Pinny came wondering to Harry Start, touching his jacket, his arm, his cheek. "You was tall," she said, "an' dark—"

"An' handsome?" he teased, uncertainly.

"You was dark," she said, "at any rate."

His daffodils squeaked and shook. I wondered where he'd got them. They were almost out of season.

"Yes," said Pinny. "Dark," said Pinny. "Black-like, in the face."

"Coal dust," said Harry Start – and he stroked his cheek. "I blacked up me face ... with coal dust."

"And why –" asked Howard Powell gently – "why would you want to do that?"

"I wan't thinking straight ... I was on'y sixteen."

"Sixteen," wondered Pinny. "You come up to me wild as an Arab."

Harry Start looked in the trees. He looked in the woods and the limekilns. "Wild," he nodded. "I *was* wild. 'Twas a long time ago now, but I ... went wild when Bowhays turned us out."

"Mrs Start found lodgings," said Margaret Bath softly, "but Harry's sisters took diphtheria shortly after, then Mrs Start did, too. Harry laboured on neighbouring farms, but—"

"Mother went downhill directly..." He gathered his voice with an effort. "The day she died, I took out Grandfer's pistol. I blacked up me face with coal dust to throw 'em off, see, anyone who saw me ... and I walked from Downlake by moonlight. I'd serve him bad, I said to myself, I'd serve him bad who'd served us worse…"

I watched Pinny anxiously, but she let him run on.

"An' I come up on devil Bowhays himself, as I thought, in the pickers at dawn… I saw the maid in the flowers, and I asked – and 'twas him. I followed to Quay with my heart like a stone … I come up step, step behind him – he was so, over the flowers. "Mr Bowhays," I says, and he turns, an' *bang!* I go and the trigger's stiff, but – *bang!* and down he goes like a ninepin in the flowers and I was taken directly…"

Howard Powell held up his hand. I watched him gratefully. "Well, well," he said, "it was all a long time ago now."

"Yes," said Harry Start. "A long time … a long time in Hardmoor."

Hardmoor Prison – that slit-eyed pile in the bleakest, most hope-forsaken part of the moor that ever went hungry for sun. Poor old Harry. Hardmoor, where those who ever escaped wished themselves further when the fog and the rain came down and twisted them lost and wet in the same hopeless hills which had coughed up Hardmoor itself, stone for dreary stone, in the days when inmates had modelled ships from bones to fill the desperate days. I knew. I'd seen them. The bone-ships, not the inmates.

Howard Powell looked from Harry to Pinny, from Pinny to Harry. He shrugged his shoulders. He couldn't cope with Hardmoor. "Shall we move on now? I'll bring the car round, we'll put in a spot of sight-seeing—"

"Here," said Pinny sharply. "We don't know about no movin' on yet. We en't doing nothin' we don't want to – are we, Harry?"

"No..." said Harry Start carefully, "we're not."

He cleared his throat. He looked at me. I stared right back. No mercy. He looked away. He looked back.

"I come here today – that is, Margaret here brought me – to say ... to say it was all on me, see? All of it. And none at all on ... on the little maid as was."

"All what?" I asked, making him say it.

Then he looked Pinny in the eye. "The blame," he said, "was all mine. I've had it on me seventy year'. And I don't want you to think no more about it."

And he gave up his flowers to Pinny. But Pinny stepped back.

"Stop long in Hardmoor?" she asked.

"Fifteen year'. Five on the prison farm. Out in thirty-one."

"Where'd'ee go then?"

"Underhill. Farmed at Underhill all the war." His stringy arms shook as he offered his flowers. It was important she took them.

But would she?

She eyed him a minute. He waited. I waited. Howard Powell waited. Janie and Margaret Bath didn't. They were over in Margaret Bath's hatchback, fussing something big out of the rear door.

"Give 'un to *him* then," said Pinny suddenly. "Go on. Give they flowers to *him*."

"Who then? Who shall I?" asked Harry, confused.

"*Him*," I said. "She means the Flower King."

"But how can I … how shall I give them to him?"

I almost felt sorry for him. There were no clues. There were only Pinny's rules, and no rule book to know them by except the jump of the moment.

"May I?" Howard Powell swept the daffodils from poor Harry Start. Then one by one he began to drop them on the water – and there they stuck, half in, half out, yellow on grey, caught on the river like jungle birds too tired to fly.

The trees stirred. Something binged against the mast, high in the rig of the *Avatar*. The Flower King took his flowers and pulled them away on the river's grand and rolling back. It was as good a way to give them to him as any.

Harry Start threw the fifth – and the sixth –

and Pinny the next. I threw the eighth – flop – on the water, in my turn. We stood, the four of us, throwing daffodils on the river. Howard Powell threw the last. We watched them roll away.

"We spent a lifetime jumpin' on some beggar else's string – an't we, Harry?" said Pinny softly, watching.

"That's right," said Harry. "We worked hard all our lives."

"What's done's done. We got to please ourselves now."

"We're pleasin' ourselves now," said Harry fiercely. "Aren't we?"

They were pleasing themselves – and what pleased them most was the daffodils drifting away like tissue on the tide.

"I told you wrong," grieved Pinny. "'Twas *me* told you wrong."

"Wrong?" said Harry. "It was *all* wrong. And don't you think no more about it."

She watched him slyly. "I won't if you won't," she said.

And I didn't think she would. It'd been a gamble, bringing them together. But Margaret Bath knew Pinny better than I did, better than she knew herself. It had been the right thing to do.

"Happy Birthday to you… " Margaret Bath and Janie came crackling up behind us with the gift-wrapped monster present they'd lugged from the car. "Happy Birthday to you... "

I knew what it was, of course. When Pinny ripped it free and saw for herself, her face showed what it meant. It meant the long and aching days in the fields with the spring wind pressing her hair and sap-glue binding her fingers. It meant bread and jam for dinner under the hedge and Mr William's careful tread in the rows. Ten thousand brilliant flowers, and a price to pay for each.

"It's called *The Last Field*," I told her. "Because it is."

There she was. Young Addie with her basket, laughing through her hair, blazed around in daffodils – and over all, the buzzard hawks in a cornflower blue sky that rolled away beyond.

"Maid o' the flowers..." rumbled Harry Start. "The very spit."

"First class, Margaret," said Howard Powell. "Don't you think so, Janie?"

"Do I *ever*," breathed Janie. "Magnif."

Howard Powell clipped off to the car park looking businesslike. It was getting time to go. No mention of Mount Hope. I wondered Pinny hadn't asked. Why hadn't she?

"I never 'ad a painting in me life," said Pinny. "I don't hardly know what to do."

"I spoke to Mrs Screech about that," said Margaret Bath. "She says your room or the day

199

lounge, over the mantelpiece, whichever you prefer."

Pinny looked greedily over her canvas. "Day lounge'd go nice." Then she sighed.

"What?" I asked.

She shook her head. "If mother could on'y see this."

Howard Powell swashed round in the car. *Geep Geeep!* He gave us the horn.

"Come on, Pinny," said Janie. "The painting'll go in the back, won't it?"

It was goodbye to Margaret Bath and Harry Start. I spread my arms and dropped them. "Things to do, places to go."

"That's all right," said Margaret. "We're going a walk now, aren't we, Harry?"

Harry Start fumbled his pocket. "I brought this." He handed me the Mini Masterbrain. "Found several pegs in me clothes. A hundred and … seven altogether. I hope I … got it right."

"Oh, yeh," I said. "You got it right this time."

His long face cracked a smile. I sent it back, with interest. No blame.

"Where you off to now, then?" he asked.

"You please yourself, Harry," called Pinny from the car.

He picked up his voice. "I said, where you off to now?"

Then she said it. The thing I'd been dreading

she'd say all along.

"Up the old place. We're goin' Mount Hope now – aren't we?"

CHAPTER
TWENTY

"A man broke down near a monastery. He went up and asked if he could stay the night, and the monks said, all right, you can. There was a big bump in the night, and in the morning the man said, what was that big bump in the night? And the monk said, you're not a monk so I can't tell you, but if you practise ten years, then I can. So the man stayed and became a monk, and at the end of ten years he said, so what was that bump in the night?" Janie Powell paused and turned to me. "What do *you* think it was?"

"I don't know. What?"

"I can't tell you," she finished lamely. "You're not a monk."

"Ha," said Howard Powell. "Ha, ha."

"What d'you get if you cross the M5 with a donkey?" I tried the worst joke I could think of. The oldest anyway.

"I don't know," said Howard Powell gamely, over his tea. "What *do* you get if you cross the M5 with a donkey?"

"Run over. Pass the sandwiches ... not them, those. Cheers."

It was an amazing spread. Tuna sandwiches (dolphin friendly, Janie said), quiche, salmon, salad with things in I'd never seen before, cream cakes, chocolate mousse – the works. Pinny ate steadily through everything on offer. She missed nothing that teatime at Stopeley but a hefty slice of home. If I could have dished up Mount Hope on a plate, I would've.

The fact was, we'd swung wide of the turning to Toy's Lane on the way back from Morden, taking in a tour of Lower Cletchley and Leigh Crags – and not a word said. I did my impression of D going off his handle – which went down well – and did a few jokes and pretended not to notice as we headed away. If Pinny noticed, she didn't make anything of it.

We drove on Clinker's Row, past the very roof that had split Black William's head; by the potteries, where once the bone-works had been; by Dingle's Shaft, by the quarry, and by Cletchley Old Mine. Pinny squawked and pointed. All the old places, changed but the same. Was she wondering when, if ever, Howard Powell would bring her home? But

Howard Powell had steered clear of Mount Hope. Why would he visit a burned-out shell? It was sticky as a jammy dodger all round.

"That's a lovely cup o' tea," said Pinny. "Teatime 'ome, mind, we'd 'ave kettle broth. An't had a drop o' kettle broth in years."

"And what," asked Howard Powell, "might kettle broth be?"

"Kettle broth, he's a dab o' stock or bacon, butter – whatever you got – an' hot water over, salt an' pepper, an' a bit o' plain bread in the top. Times I told Screech, but she won't do me up no kettle broth."

"I'll try'n make you some if you like," offered Janie.

"Don't trouble now, dear," said Pinny. "I was only tellin' teatime 'ome. Tell of that, me an' Dorothy – that's me sister – me an' Dorothy'd go butcher, and we'd 'ave a basket between us, an' catch hold one each side. And we'd 'ave a bullock's head in the basket, an' come 'ome, all down Terrace with that old head eye lookin' up at us. And Mother, she made brawn, and 'e'd last all week."

"A bullock's head? In a basket?" Janie Powell wrinkled her nose.

The dining room was bright with fancy mirrors either end. Its casement windows took up half of the front of the house – the other half was William's Kennel. The tone was chocolate brown. It was the only room I'd seen which had had a lick of paint this century. The bushes outside clacked against the windows. The wind was up. The sky looked ugly beyond.

"Looks like rain," said Janie. Then she said, "Bet there's windows open upstairs."

"Yes," said Howard Powell. "I'll just nip up and shut them. I don't like the look of the weather."

When he'd gone, I wandered out. I crossed to William's Kennel. I pushed the door. I went in.

I went straight to the Flower King. Margaret Bath's *View Over Stopeley* beside him was wild with her dashing strokes, strong where strong was needed, where the house cut the lawns in clean and careful lines. Black William was gone for ever. If I never saw him again, it'd be too soon.

I almost stood on the dog. It was asleep on the rug in a blonde heap of hair so much like a rug itself it was asking to be stepped on. It looked up. It flopped its tail once or twice and settled its nose on its paws. I remembered it wouldn't come in the room at all, back along. Now there was a dog in the Kennel, in place of something wilder.

The Flower King looked down. Sorry, I told him. Never mind the dog. It was you I came to see.

The door twitched. Pinny looked round. "Where's the lav to, dear?"

"Down the hall, I think. Come in a minute."

"Shall I, then?"

"Come in. Mind the dog."

She came in slowly, like the new kid in school. "I an't never been in the 'ouse before."

"Didn't Mr William bring you?"

She reached the Flower King and blinked up. I looked, and Pinny looked. He was different for each of us, but altogether himself. I brought her, see, I told him, in my head. It's all right now. All of it. The lovely still blue light around him, I knew, was only a blink away – just as it had been at Morden, when the flowers had flopped on the water and the river had rolled them away. Deep peace. Refuge, where refuge was home.

"He was, he was just the same's that," said Pinny softly. "Just exac'ly the same's that. You'd never've known it to see him."

"Known what?"

"Oh, well. He wan't a well man, he 'ad the whatchamacallit, coughin' red an' that—"

She stopped to listen – a rumble, deep in the house, or over it. Thunder over Stopeley. I rushed in the hall, expecting I didn't know what – but it was only Howard Powell taking the stairs like a fall of rubble. His eyes were bright, his hair wild. He held a thick green file against his chest.

"The most extraordinary thing – I can't imagine why…"

"Pinny!" I called. We followed slowly to the dining room. It looked like he'd found the – well, it could have been the—

"The Mount Hope file! And the Bowhays journal! On Mrs Teagarden's bed!" He clapped it on the table between the potato salad and the dish of cream. "I nipped in to shut the window – and there it was. Why in heaven's name would Gaye leave these in her room? Why would she hide them in the first place?"

I flashed to Janie Powell. She looked up coolly over the mousse bowl. "Funny, isn't it?" she said. "Funny woman, really. Those awful hats."

I caught her eye. Nice one, I grinned. Planting the stuff on the absent Mrs T. had a neatness about it that appealed to me. Pretty neat all round, really. But Howard Powell wasn't listening to Janie. He was scanning a bunch of typewritten documents in the back of the Mount Hope file.

"Confirmation of purchase… Ah! The insurance policy! Thank God!"

I tweaked out the leatherbound journal. Anything to switch the subject from *what* was insured, and why. It was good to feel the journal's heaviness again, to smell its old-book smell, to look all I wanted in its spider-leg text.

"Pinny, look, see this?" I showed her the name in the spotted flyleaf, but she couldn't see for looking. "See? William Arthur Bowhays Johns. January 1912. It's the Flower King's journal."

"Well, now. There's a thing."

It was more than a thing. It was his living voice on the page. I picked out an entry at random.

"Twenty-seventh March. 'By first-class despatch this morning, to Messrs Draycott & Gidding, Purveyors of Fruit & Flowers, Covent Garden, confirmation of my visit next month. By hand, my hope to Reverend Spicer that all go forward speedily with commencement of the Methodist Chapel, the foundation stone being already engraved with such name and date as will hold me to account for ever should I be unable to lay it. Dr Courtnay gives me good hope that I shall.'"

I paused, disappointed. "What's it mean?"

Howard Powell took up the journal. "Yes, it appears he was quite ill. In this entry he worries about being well enough to lay the foundation stone at the Chapel—"

"Tuberculosis!" said Pinny suddenly. "That's – yes – that's what Mr William had. He had the TB, and Dr Courtnay was one o' they upcountry doctors."

Howard Powell flicked through the entries. "Thirteenth of April. 'Father bears down on his tenants, I fear. He will not tend the vine, but must pluck out the fruit and crush the plant beneath his heel. He will presently consume Start's Meadow, and all the land adjoining.'"

"Harry Start's father dies," put in Janie excitedly. "Old William schemes to evict the family."

"Just so," said Howard Powell. "He goes on: 'In Father's absence my dearest Lilian—'"

"Who's Lilian?" I asked.

"Lilian Bodrugan," said Pinny. "Lilian Bodrugan as was engaged to marry young Mr William, but she never."

"So ... his fiancée, Lilian – where was I? – 'In Father's absence my dearest Lilian has proposed a revival of the Tenants' Cup, or Feast, in the Long Barn, that we may show a neighbourly face and meet with all those tenants with whom the family has never been personally acquainted.'"

"If he *met* everyone," I said, "how come Harry Start didn't know who he was?"

"But he never *did* meet everyone. He goes on: 'Arrangements well advanced for Tenants' Cup' – no ... where are we now?" Howard Powell leafed on impatiently. "Here we are. Listen to this: May the eighth. 'I have left Father raging in the Kennel. It is all up with the Tenants' Feast. Father's horse throwing a shoe and occasioning him a fall, his unexpected return from Exeter on the eve of the Tenants' Cup, discovered Lilian and I instructing Hatch— '"

"Hatch?" asked Janie.

"Butler Hatch," nodded Pinny.

"'Instructing Hatch for the celebrations. But it is not to be; Father tells me he will entertain nothing of the kind. All that I have done must be undone – and that, speedily. My dearest Lilian is certain it will be undutiful in me to pursue the matter. Such a look she gave me as she left the Kennel! I cannot prevail against Father. Ah, dear Lilian.'"

"The Tenants' Feast never came off," said Janie.

"Unfortunately for some, it didn't." Howard Powell peeled off his glasses and wiped them thoughtfully.

"And if it *had*," I said slowly, "an' if it *had* an' they *had* invited everyone they didn't know, then they'd have met – boy Harry and the Flower King – and he'd've seen there were *two* Mr Williams."

"Why would he?" asked Janie.

"He couldn't hardly *not* see. That's the point. Young Mr William'd introduce himself; boy Harry'd have seen he was only the son who did flowers and wanted to smooth things over."

"And," said Janie, "*and* he'd have realized the William Bowhays Johns who ran the estate was the father, the one everyone grumbled about, who—"

"Turned people out. And it wouldn't have gone all wrong like it did."

"It's precisely because William the Elder was the kind of man he was that he didn't want to face his tenants," said Howard Powell. "And it's because the Flower King was in the wrong place at the wrong time that he paid for it, I'm afraid."

I was wondering why the Flower King couldn't've had his feast anyway if he'd wanted to. And if he'd wanted to meet all the tenants, why couldn't he've ridden round to see 'em? Then again, why would he bother? How was *he* to know how important it would be, one day, to be known for who he was?

I said, "Bit weak, wasn't he? Young Mister?"

"Perhaps he'd have been disinherited or something if he'd gone against his father," shrugged Howard Powell. "Who knows?"

"Young Mister, he din' care for nothin' but they flower fields, not reelly," sniffed Pinny. "Never *did* marry."

The wind rattled the windows. Janie stared in the potato salad and smoothed it with a teaspoon. Pinny swirled her tea leaves and sucked in her cheeks. Everyone was still, thinking about what had and might have been.

Howard Powell stirred. "He finishes with: 'I must have a fine basket of strawberries for Mr Draycott on the twentieth, having assured him of three weeks' advantage in the purchase of Valley strawberries over any other supplier in the market. Dr Courtnay insists on Egypt or Morocco this September, but there is much that remains to be done.'"

"Why Egypt?" I asked.

"For the climate. Standard treatment for TB for the well-to-do. Fascinating, isn't it?"

"Poor Mr William," said Janie Powell. "He didn't have long to live."

"Went on three year' well enough," said Pinny gruffly. "Went on well enough till Harry Start did a bit o' doctorin'."

The Flower King had tended the vine, and where had it got him? If he'd outlived Black William, I couldn't help thinking, how different things might have been.

"Oh!" Janie Powell covered her mouth. "I almost forgot! Dad – come on."

"Come on what?"

"In the kitchen. *You* know."

"Yes. I believe I do." Howard Powell snapped the journal shut. He stood up. "Won't be a tick. Talk amongst yourselves."

There were three ticks of the marble clock precisely. When they brought in the cake, we'd hardly time to sort a plate each to eat it off. It was a layered sponge-and-cream job topped in kiwi fruit. In the centre, in silver numbers, was a giant 85. Around it were eight white candles – one for each of Pinny's ten years –

and one white half-a-candle, for the half-a-decade, on top.

"Lush," I said. "Who made it?"

"We both did, didn't we, Dad?" said Janie, with her face glowing in the lighted candles.

"We conjured up all of this, Janie and I," said Howard Powell. "Marvellous morning in the kitchen."

"Organic flour only, wasn't it, Dad?" glowed Janie.

"What else?" he asked, putting one big arm round her.

I watched them together whilst Pinny blew her candles. Janie winked at me, once – or was it the smoke? Eat your heart out, Mrs Teagarden. Janie Rules, OK?

"Wish then, Pinny," I urged her. "You didn't wish. Go on. You've got to wish."

"I can't think of nothin'."

"Go on. Just – *wish*. Anything."

"I wish," said Pinny wistfully, "I wish I could find the lav."

CHAPTER TWENTY-ONE

"Well," said Howard Powell grimly. "Got to check the damage sometime, I suppose. Might as well be now."

He swung left on Toy's Lane with a twitch of his wrist on the wheel. We were homeward to Needham's at six forty-five. Supposed to be, anyway.

"Is now a good time?" I glanced back at Pinny.

"Doesn't she know?" He shrugged. "She'll have to know sometime."

I forgave him. He didn't really know how much it meant. I checked Pinny again in the back. But she didn't pick up on it at all.

She sat watching the hedges slide by as though she weren't about to have twenty years of her life snuffed out on a heap of steaming beams. What would she say when she saw

Mount Hope in ruins? How would she feel, after all Mount Hope had meant, after all I'd promised? I felt like jumping out of the car and legging it over the hill, somewhere I wouldn't have to show an old friend the empty grate their memories were.

Giant raindrops plopped on the windscreen. The wipers slicked them away. We nosed down over the ruts.

I watched her face as Mount Hope came in view. The charred walls, the scorched field, the blasted garden. It could have been worse – but I couldn't see how.

"I'll just take a quick look." Howard Powell whacked on the handbrake and slammed out.

Pinny was fiddling with the door-catch, blindly. I jumped out and helped her. I had a lump in my throat the size of Tarmouth.

"Where's your hat? Pinny. Put your hat on."

I fixed her up with her walking frame. We skirted the gate – end up in the lane – and edged in the gap it had guarded.

It was an awesome sight. The ends of blackened roof-beams stuck out between the gable ends like spoons in a pot. The roof had brought a lot more down with it than the chimney. Half of the top of the front wall had packed up as well. The doorless front doorway had gagged on slates and thrown them up in the garden. A stack more slates balanced dangerously on the flame-cracked lintels above.

Somewhere under half a ton of rubble lay the black and smoking kitchen. What was left of the walls above the downstairs windows streamed soot-marks up to meet empty air where once the bedrooms had been.

For the moment, Mount Hope was still. Everything that was going to fall had fallen. Everything that hadn't was holding – just. The rain hissed in. There was nothing, any more, to stop it.

Howard Powell had disappeared off up the field for an overview. But any way you looked at it, it was a pig's ear of a steaming, burnt-out, churned-up, mashed-over mess.

I looked at Pinny as we stood in the mud, crisscrossed with hose-casts and firemen's boot prints. She wouldn't improve in the rain. I cleared my throat to begin.

"I was going to tell you, but—"

"I knowed," said Pinny softly. "I knowed all along 'e was gone."

"You did?"

"'Ad it from Elaine this morning. She 'ad it from Constable Dent."

"Pinny," I said. "I'm so sorry."

"What's to be sorry for? You give me a lovely day out."

"You wanted to see it so much, and now…"

She flipped a slate with her foot. "Roof never was no good. Ground's best place for 'un."

Nothing I could say would make any difference at all. The space between us grew. What could I say to fill it?

"Look. One of those scoot things."

I spotted a dim half-circle under a heap of slates. I picked it up quickly – and dropped it again twice as fast. "Woh, that's *hot*."

The ends of my fingers were shiny and dead-feeling. Where I'd touched the scoot my fingerprints'd gone. Suddenly it hurt a lot. I looked around. No sign of Howard Powell.

"Look," I told Pinny, "you're getting wet. There's nothing to see. I think you should get in the car. I'll go and—"

"Find Johnnie Gently? Take me up Screech's again?"

"Don't you want to go back up Needham's?"

Her wet hat brushed my face. "I won't be stoppin' long at Screech's, no," she whispered. "Not long up Screech's now."

What this was supposed to mean, I didn't know. But I went to find John Gently just the same.

I found him round the back. "Rebuild job," he said glumly. "Only thing worth salvaging's the old Cornish range. I was planning to make it a feature."

"Oh, well," I shrugged. "Clean slate, isn't it? Here. I found this."

I handed him the sign off the gate, the sign

that said Mount Hope.

He looked at it thoughtfully. "Thanks, Graham. It *is* mine, gutted or not. Sometimes I have the strangest feeling it isn't."

"All yours," I said, as though it were mine to give. "Now."

He nodded. He closed his hand on the sign. Something had truly passed from one hand to another.

"I think we better get Mrs Pinder home. Else," I joked weakly, "she might move back in."

It wasn't as weak as I thought. She wasn't where I'd left her. She wasn't in the car.

"Pinny!" I called, "where are you?"

Right smack in the centre of the rubble was where she was. How did she get there? Right in under the hair-trigger slates, on the blackened break-a-leg floor.

"Pinny, come out! It's not safe!"

"No one c'n put 'un back as he was," she was telling herself over and over and over – not sadly, really, at all. "No, no one'll put 'un back. Not like 'e was. Not even Johnnie Gently. No one'll ever—"

"He *can*," I shouted crazily. "John Gently can do *anything*."

"Cos on'y I know how 'e was, see? That's, yes, that's where Father got his chair in the draught again – over by the door. That you, Dor'thy? Door's gone, see? Well. Don't need

218

no door to see where Father's chair was. Don't need no wall, don't need no floor. See I got it all in me 'ead I have, an' I won't never forget. I won't never, never…"

Suddenly I knew what hope really was. Just before Howard Powell went in after her, something happened. Pinny smiled, the calmest smile you'd see in a million years; and out of that smile a white light grew, the loveliest light I'd ever seen. It grew until it filled me.

And I knew. Pinny was coming home.

WEATHER EYE

Lesley Howarth

Telly Craven is a Weather Eye, part of a club that shares information by computer about climatic conditions around the world. And, as 1999 ends, weird things are happening: floods, earthquakes, force ten gales... It's during such a storm that Telly has a Near Death Experience, leaving her with strange psychic powers. Now she is *the* Weather Eye with a clear, if daunting purpose...

"Often very funny... It is subtle, sophisticated and beautifully written... It must reinforce Lesley Howarth's position as one of the best novelists now writing for young readers." *Gillian Cross, The Times Educational Supplement*

"Outstanding... A degree of suspense and pace that would do credit to Raymond Chandler." *The Independent*

MAPHEAD

Lesley Howarth

Greetings from the Subtle World –

Twelve-year-old MapHead is a visitor from the Subtle World that exists side by side with our own. Basing himself in a tomato house, the young traveller has come to meet his mortal mother for the first time. But, for all his dazzling alien powers, can MapHead master the language of the human heart?

"Weird, moving and funny by turns... Lesley Howarth has a touch of genius."
Chris Powling, Books for Keeps

"Offbeat and original... Strongly recommended to all who enjoy a good story."
Books For Your Children

Winner of the 1995 Guardian Children's Fiction Award

MISTER SPACEMAN

Lesley Howarth

Thomas Moon is a space freak. His room's done up like the Mir Space Station. He hunts the websites daily for space news and stories. He wants to be an astronaut. And according to the mysterious email he's just received, addressed to Mister Spaceman, his dreams are about to come true...

"Each of her books is an invigorating display of verbal fireworks, and a fresh foray into the imagination."
Gillian Cross, TES

MORE WALKER PAPERBACKS
For You to Enjoy